NOBLE BEGINNINGS

THE JACK NOBLE SERIES™ BOOK ONE

L.T. RYAN

LIQUID MIND MEDIA

Jack Noble™ and The Jack Noble Series™ are trademarks of L.T. Ryan and Liquid Mind Media, LLC.

ISBN: 978-1-68533-011-8

For information contact:

contact@ltryan.com

https://LTRyan.com

https://www.instagram.com/ltryanauthor/

https://www.facebook.com/LTRyanAuthor

THE JACK NOBLE SERIES

For paperback purchase links, visit:
https://ltryan.com/jack-noble

BAGHDAD, IRAQ. MARCH, 2002

I LEANED BACK AGAINST A WEATHERED STONE WALL. MUFFLED VOICES SLIPPED through the cracked door. The night air felt cool against my sweat-covered forehead. A light breeze carried with it the smell of raw sewage. Orange-tinted smoke from a distant fire rose high into the sky. Wisps of smoke streaked across the full moon ahead of the mass of artificial cloud cover, threatening to block the moonlight I used to keep watch over the sleepy street while the CIA special operations team did their job inside the house. The smart team leaders kept me involved. The dumb ones left me outside to guard the entrance.

Eight years on the job. Best gig I ever had. Then Bin Laden attacked the U.S. Forty-eight hours later everything had changed. Most teams were deployed to Afghanistan. Bear and I were sent to Iraq. We'd spent six months raiding houses just like this one inside and on the outskirts of Baghdad. And just like tonight, we were kept outside the house.

The only connection we had with the Marine Corps was the ten Marines over here with us. We only saw them a couple times a week. I had no idea where the rest of our Marine brethren were, and I didn't care. They didn't consider us Marines any more than we considered them brethren.

"Jack?" Bear said.

Bear had been my partner and best friend since our last day of recruit training. A recruit training experience cut four weeks short.

"Yeah," I said.

"I'm tired of this."

I turned my head, keeping my M16 aimed forward. Bear stared out into the distance. The faint orange glow of the fire cloud reflected off the sheen of sweat across his face.

"They just keep us posted outside," he said. "Ain't never treated us like this."

I shrugged. He was right. But there was nothing we could do about it. Bear and I were on loan to the CIA and had to do whatever we were told. Before 9/11, we were part of the team. But the CIA agents we normally worked with stayed behind in the U.S. and Europe. The teams over here weren't used to having two Marines with them and they weren't receptive to the idea.

"What do you suggest we do?" I said. "Quit?"

Bear shook his head and straightened his six foot six body. He shifted his rifle in his hands and walked toward the end of the house. Beyond his large frame I spotted a group of men. Figured that was why Bear went on high alert.

There were six of them huddled together. They spoke in whispers and appeared to look in our direction. Another three men walked toward the group. From this distance they didn't appear to be armed, but they had the cover of night on their side. Best to assume they were prepared to wreak havoc on our position.

"What do you make of that?" I asked.

Bear looked back at me with narrowed eyes and a clenched jaw.

"Trouble."

Trouble lingered everywhere in this damn city. No one trusted us here. Every time I turned a corner I worried someone would be standing there waiting to take me out. The only person I could trust in Iraq was Bear. The CIA spec ops teams we'd been attached to looked down on us. They all seemed to be waiting for the right moment to drop us. Hell, for all I knew, they were inside that house negotiating our arrest.

Bear cleared his throat and then pointed toward the group. The nine men fanned out and began approaching our position. The sound of their voices rose from a murmur to light chatter. I made out distinct sounds. Despite being in Iraq for the past six months, I had a weak grasp on the language.

"What are they saying?" I asked.

Bear held up his hand, fingers outstretched. He cocked his head like he was looking up at the moon. His body crouched into a defensive position. The barrel of the M16 rose to waist level. He reached out with his left hand to steady the rifle. I did the same. The A3 was a much better option for security teams than the Marine standard issue A4. We could drop the entire group of men in under five seconds if we chose to do so.

"Talk to me, Bear," I said.

He took three slow steps back, blocking my view of part of the street. He yelled something in Arabic.

The group stopped their advance. One man stepped forward. His tall, gangly body stood out from the short stocky men in the group. He lifted his arms, a handgun clutched in his right hand. I tensed and tapped my finger against the M16's trigger. The harsh sounds of words spoken in Arabic filled the air. They echoed through the street. Then silence penetrated.

Bear turned to look at me, then smiled, then looked back at the men. He shouted in Arabic again and lifted his M16 to his shoulder.

The tall Iraqi raised his arms once again. He had put his gun away. He turned his back to us, said something to the group of men and started walking away. The mob held their positions for a moment. The tall man pushed past them. He spoke in an authoritative tone, his voice rising to a yell. They turned and followed him. A few looked back over their shoulders in our direction.

I exhaled loudly. Cool, calm and collected when others would panic. Now, however, I felt my hands trembling slightly. A deep breath reset me to normal. It was a typical sequence of events.

"Christ, Bear. What the hell was that about?"

He chuckled. "I think they're on our side, Jack."

"What makes you think that?" I used my sleeve to wipe a layer of cold sweat from my brow.

His smile widened. "They didn't shoot."

"What did you say to them... ah, forget it. You're a crazy SOB. You know that, right?"

He shrugged, ignoring me and scanning darkened windows.

I leaned back against the wall, joined him. "You think this is what Keller had in mind when he shipped us off to the CIA?"

I had kept in touch with General Keller since he took us out of recruit training and placed us into the CIA sponsored program some eight years ago. I knew this was not what he had in mind.

Bear said, "Beats what we'd be doing otherwise."

I threw my head back and nodded over my shoulder toward the door. "You sure about that?"

Bear shrugged. His big head shook slightly. He wiped his face and then looked at me.

"I'm not sure of much anymore, Jack. This is what I know. They ship us somewhere. We do our job. Pretty simple."

I nodded. It was pretty simple. Eight years now and we knew the routine. We do our job. Only here, our job had been castrated down to nothing but a security detail while they did the work that would get the glory. Hopefully they'd get it soon and ship us back to the U.S.

We stood in silence. I stared at the orange glow of the cloud that covered half the sky.

"Noble. Logan."

The voice ripped through the air like a mortar arcing over our heads. The door whipped open. Bealle stood in the doorway.

"We need you two inside."

I turned to face Eddie Bealle, fourth man on the totem pole of the four-man CIA spec ops team. "We're ready to go, Bealle."

WE FOLLOWED Bealle through the narrow doorway and down an even narrower hallway. The smell of burned bread filled the house. I looked over my shoulder and saw Bear shuffling sideways behind me, his broad shoulders too wide to fit square between the thin plaster walls. We turned a corner to another stretch of hall that opened up to a dimly lit room.

"What's the deal here, Bealle?" I asked.

Bealle said nothing. He just kept walking. His rank on the team was too low to justify acting like a prick. I had wanted the opportunity to beat it out of him for weeks now. He stepped through the opening, walked across the room and rejoined his team.

I followed, stopped and stepped to the right. Bear stepped to the left.

Scott Martinez looked over and nodded. He said something in Arabic to the Iraqi man sitting on the floor. The man's arms and legs were bound with the thick plastic ties we carried. Martinez rose from his crouching position and walked toward me. He ran a hand through his sweat-soaked short brown hair and wiped blood spatter off his cheek. He stopped a few feet in front of me. Like most spec op guys, he was a good four inches shorter than me and a head shorter than Bear. There were exceptions. My eyes drifted across the room and locked on Aaron Kiser. He stood six foot two and could look me directly in the eye.

I scanned the room, my eyes inching along the yellow stained walls and ceiling. Paintings and family photos hung crooked in obvious spots. The furniture had been pushed to the far end of the room. The captive family huddled together at the other end. The man stared blankly at the floor between his bound feet. His wife sat behind him, her black hair frizzed and disheveled. Blood trickled from the corner of her mouth. Her hands rested in her lap, bound at the wrists. Hiding behind her were two small children, one boy and one girl. Their scared faces peeked over her shoulder. Their eyes were dark with fear and darted between the men holding their family captive.

I hated this part of the job. If we had something on the man, fine. He likely did something to bring us here. But why keep the family held up like this? It seemed to be the MO over here lately, at least when working with Martinez. And I had no choice but to go with it.

"Your job here," Martinez said, as if he had read my mind, "is to provide support. No different than any other day. I give an order, you follow. Understand?"

I shifted my eyes to his and said nothing.

Bear coughed and crossed his arms across his chest.

Martinez dropped his head and shook it. A grin formed on his lips, but his eyes narrowed. We'd butted heads more than once, and I figured he had become as sick of me as I was of him.

"I'm so tired of you two Jarheads."

I looked over at Bear and mouthed the phrase "Jarheads" at him. He laughed.

The bound man on the floor looked up. His glassed-over eyes made contact with mine. I felt my smile fade and my lips thinned. The man's eyes burned with hatred and desperation. He took a deep breath, and then looked down at the floor.

"Follow, Noble." Martinez turned and held up his hand while gesturing toward me. He walked across the room and stopped in front of the Iraqi man and then kicked him in the stomach.

The man fell forward into Martinez's legs. His face contorted into a pained expression while he struggled to fill his lungs with air.

"Get this bastard off of me," Martinez said.

Kiser stepped forward, grabbed the Iraqi by the back of his head and dragged him to the middle of the room.

Martinez moved to the middle and crouched down. He looked the Iraqi man in the eyes.

"I want you to see this. See what your failure to give us any information has led to."

Martinez stood and walked over to the man's wife. He reached under her arm and yanked her to her feet. She gasped, and her children cried out. They grabbed at her with their tiny hands. Bealle and Richard Gallo led the woman by her elbows to the wall across from me. Martinez followed. He stood in front of the woman, leaned in and whispered in her ear.

Her eyes scanned the room and met mine. A tear rolled down her thin face. Her mouth opened slightly. Her lips quivered. She bit her bottom lip and then mouthed the word "please" to me. Martinez brought a hand to her cheek, and she started crying.

Martinez moved to his right and looked over his shoulder at the man on the floor.

"Isn't your wife worth it?" His face lit up as he said it, and his eyes grew wide and the corners of his mouth turned upwards in a sadistic grin. I noticed his respirations increased fivefold. The spec ops leader appeared to find the exchange exhilarating.

The Iraqi man said nothing. He held his head high and his shoulders back. He stood defiant on his knees.

Martinez brushed the woman's hair back behind her ears and leaned in toward her again and whispered something to her. She let out a loud sob and then took a deep breath to compose herself. She looked toward her children and said something in Arabic, and then she turned to Martinez and spit in his face.

He stepped back and used the back of his hand to wipe his face. Then he struck her with the same hand. Her head jerked back and hit the wall with a thud. Her body slumped to the floor. Martinez reached out with one hand and grabbed her by the neck and with his other hand he pulled his pistol from its holster, pressing the black gun barrel against the side of her head. His hand slid up from her neck and squeezed her cheeks in. The pressure of his hands against the sides of her face jarred her mouth open. He jammed the barrel of the gun in her mouth.

"Is this what you want?" He paused a moment. "Huh? Want your kids to see your brains blown all over this wall?"

I felt rage build. This was wrong in every sense of the word. I took a step forward. Bear's large hand came down on my shoulder and held me back.

"Get the kids out of the room, Martinez," I said.

Martinez straightened up and cocked his head. His arms dropped to his side, and then he turned to face me. He stared at me for a few seconds and lifted a finger in my direction. The woman slid down the wall and crawled on the floor to her kids.

"Noble," he said. "I told you that you follow my orders. Not the other way around. You got it?"

"Let," I took a step forward, "the kids," another step, "leave the room." I kept moving forward until we met chest to chest and eyes to chin.

I heard weapons drawn around the room and the floor creaking behind me, a sign that Bear was moving into position.

"Gallo," Martinez said.

"Yeah?" Gallo said, stepping out of the shadowy corner he had occupied.

"Move the man to the corner, then the woman," Martinez said.

Gallo did as instructed. The family huddled together in the far corner of the room.

"Now stay here, Gallo," Martinez said. "Rest of you outside. Now."

I felt the barrel of a gun in my back but didn't turn to see who it was.

"You two leave your weapons behind," Martinez said.

We moved back through the narrow hall to the slightly wider doorway. Bear stepped outside first, I went second, and Kiser came out behind me with Bealle and finally Martinez in tow.

The moon now hovered directly above the street, beyond the cover of the orange smoke. I scanned the street and spotted a group of men hanging out a few blocks away. Were they the same men from earlier or perhaps a new group of men not as friendly as the last? Their chatter stopped. They turned to face us. A few of them stepped forward. Were they planning to attack? That wouldn't be a bad thing, of course. It might give us and the CIA spec ops something in common to fight, instead of each other.

"You guys keep an eye on him," Martinez said.

I swung my head around and saw Kiser and Bealle aim their guns on Bear. Like us, they carried Beretta M9 9mm pistols. Weapon of choice, it seemed. I followed Martinez's movements as he paced a five foot area in the middle of the street.

"Noble," Martinez said. "Step on out here."

I looked at Bear, and he nodded in return, and then winked. I crossed the packed dirt yard and stepped into the street.

Martinez lunged at me the moment my foot hit the pavement.

I ducked his blow and followed up by pushing his back. His momentum sent him into the side of the house. He reached out with his arms and came to a grinding halt. He turned, rolled his head. His neck and shoulders cracked and popped.

Kiser and Bealle kept their weapons pointed at Bear, but their eyes were fixed on Martinez.

I made the next move and engaged Martinez. We danced in a tight spiral, trading blows of fist and foot. Every connection sent a cloudburst of sweat and blood into the air. The two of us struck and countered with the precision of two highly trained prize fighters. We were equals now.

Martinez threw a flurry of punches. One landed on the side of my head. The blow knocked me to the ground. I knew his next move would be to kick me in the midsection. I quickly rolled and got to my hands and feet.

Martinez backed up.

I looked to the side. Saw black combat boots less than four feet away. I didn't have to look up to know the boots didn't belong to Bear. He wore brown boots.

Martinez started toward me. I had to time my attack just right. If I struck too soon Martinez would be out of my reach. Too late and he'd be upon me before I would have a chance to react.

I took a deep breath as time slowed down. Martinez's boots hit the packed dirt, heel then toe, left then right. He was ten feet way, then eight, then six.

I launched into the air to the right and twisted my body. Kiser didn't have time to react other than to turn slightly toward me. His outstretched right arm moved too slowly. My body continued to twist to the right, and I whipped my left arm around. My hand wrapped into a fist and struck Kiser's windpipe hard and fast. He let out a loud gasp as the impact caused him to drop his gun. His hands went to his neck as he stumbled backward and fell to the ground. He tried to suck air into his lungs, but his crushed throat wouldn't allow it. His lungs shriveled and his face turned red, then blue, and scrunched up into a contorted look of agony.

Martinez closed the gap between the two of us. It was the right move at the wrong time. What he should have done was pulled his weapon. Again, I ducked and slipped to the side, letting his momentum carry him a good ten feet away from me.

I cast a quick glance toward Bear, who held Bealle's limp body against the building with his left hand while his right delivered punch after furious punch.

With Bealle and Kiser out of commission, I turned to deal with Martinez, who had just scraped himself off the ground and was approaching. I still couldn't figure out why he didn't pull his gun on me. End it quickly. He stepped over Kiser's limp body, coming to a stop a few feet away from me.

I heard a body hit the ground behind me and then Bear appeared next to me.

Martinez lunged forward. I moved to the side and brought a fist down across the bridge of his nose, sending him to the ground, hard. Bear picked him up, and then drove two hard blows to the man's face and then tossed him onto the ground next to Bealle.

We reentered the house with our guns drawn and confronted Gallo. He gave up without a fight.

"You people should leave," I said to the family. "Tonight. Now."

Bear removed the thick plastic ties that bound their arms together.

The family huddled together. Each parent scooped up a kid.

"Follow us out and then go." I grabbed my M16 from its resting spot on the wall and then led the family down the narrow hall. I stopped by the door, took a deep breath and then stuck my head outside. It was deserted. Martinez and his men and even the group of Iraqi men down the street had bailed. I saw flashing lights reflecting off the surrounding buildings as sirens filled the air.

"Bear," I called down the hall. "We need to get out of here."

2

Martinez and the others peeled away in the van we had ridden in. That left Bear and me searching for a way back to headquarters. But first, we had to get away from the house before the police arrived. We managed to slip around the corner prior to a squad car arriving.

"You pay attention on the ride in?" I asked.

Bear nodded. "I've been out here before."

I scanned the street. Empty, except for a few small cars parked on narrow strips of dirt between the road and houses.

"Take your pick."

He pointed at a blue two door that didn't look like it could fit one of us, let alone both of us. He started toward the car parked a half block away. The sound of driving slowly echoed from behind.

"We better pick it up," I said.

We reached the car. Both of us were ready to smash in the windows. I checked the door handle and found it to be unlocked. We got inside just before white light flooded the street. I looked back and saw a police car at the end of the road with its spotlight pointing in our direction. Bear pulled at the cheap plastic underneath the steering column and ripped it free. He touched the ignition wires together and the little car buzzed to life. He put it in first gear and we rolled to the end of the street. Anticipation and anxiety filled the front of the car. We stopped at the end of the road. The floodlight still illuminated the street. It didn't get closer, didn't fade away.

"Turn left," I said.

"We need to go right."

"I'm sure we can pick it back up, Bear. But let's go left, circle back and see what these guys are doing."

He nodded, eased the car forward and made a left turn. The shift from bright light to darkness messed with our vision and we almost didn't notice the group of men in the road.

Bear hit the brakes. "Really?" He pounded on the horn. Short bursts of high-pitched honks filled the air. "Doesn't anybody hang out in a bar in this damn country?"

"Flash your highs and move slow, Bear."

He did.

The group of men split in the middle, just enough for us to pass between the divided group. They leaned over and peered through the window. A few pushed against the small car, rocking it on its chassis.

"I got a bad feeling, Jack."

"Just keep going."

I clutched my Beretta M9 tight against my chest, ready to fire on the first man to punch through the window. The M16s were lying across the back seat. A chill washed over me at the thought of one or two of the men getting into the back of the car and getting their hands on the fully automatic weapons. One squeeze of the trigger and they could take us and half their group out before they realized they had fired.

The car slowed to a stop.

"What the hell, Bear?"

"Want me to run him over?" He flung his arms forward.

I opened my mouth to say yes and turned my head to look out the windshield. A small kid, maybe seven or eight years old, stood directly in our path.

"Put it in reverse."

Bear's eyes darted to the rearview mirror.

"They're blocking the path."

I turned in my seat to get a look at the gathering of men behind us. Three silhouettes blocked the moonlit view of the street.

"Run them over."

"What?"

"They put themselves there," I said. "They have a choice. That kid didn't."

Bear's hand moved to the shifter. He slid it over then down, into reverse. Hit the gas. Three quick thuds filled the car. Two men fell to the side. The car bounced as we rolled over the third.

The rest of the men separated and we sped backward. They regrouped and huddled around their injured friend. A few turned their attention toward us and then bottles and rocks rained down on the little car.

Bear whipped the car around in a tight circle. Threw it into first then sped away in the opposite direction. I kept my head turned and watched through the back window for nearly five minutes.

"I think we're good."

Bear nodded, checking the rearview mirror every three to five seconds. "It's getting too hot, Jack."

"I know. I don't like this any more than you."

I leaned back in my undersized seat, rubbed my eyes with my thumbs, then turned my head and stared out the window. We were outside the city, past the suburbs. The barren landscape was a welcome respite from the hordes of roaming vigilantes and anti-American Iraqis we encountered on a daily basis.

"I'll call Abbot and Keller after we get back. See about getting us out of here."

Bear didn't say anything. His big hands wrapped around the steering wheel, his eyes focused on the empty road. We rode in silence the remaining twenty miles back to base.

WE SHARED a single room on base. Two single beds, a small kitchenette with a stove, mini-fridge and microwave, and a wooden table with two matching chairs. Frankly, we didn't need much else. We ate, slept, trained on our own and performed missions with the CIA ops teams. Outside of the missions, the operatives had no interaction with us. It wasn't a written rule or anything like that. They didn't want anything to do with us. These guys looked down on the Marines in the program. A stark contrast from the operatives based in the U.S. and Europe. They welcomed the help and our point of view on the missions. Christ, they pulled us eight weeks into recruit training, and we were then put through CIA training. It's not like Bear and I were hardcore Marines.

Bear returned to the room carrying a twelve pack of piss warm beer.

"Get anything to eat?" I asked.

He held up the twelve pack. "Figured it's a good night to drink our dinner."

"Only problem with that," I said, "is six beers doesn't make a meal."

He stepped through the doorway and into the room then lifted his other arm. "That's why I got you your own."

I laughed, then grabbed the cardboard box holding my dinner and cracked open a warm one, taking a long pull from the bottle.

"God, this stuff is awful," I said.

Bear chugged three quarters of a bottle then set it down on the table and let out a loud exhale.

"I don't know, Jack. It's not that bad." A loud belch followed.

I finished my beer and pushed back from the table. "And with that, I'm going to get a shower."

I exited the room into the dimly lit hallway. It was quiet. I checked my watch and saw it was only ten p.m. It was too quiet for ten, though. I shook my head to clear the thoughts and shrugged off the anxiety. I entered the bathroom and shower facility at our end of the hall, finding the communal shower room empty. I quickly washed the sweat, dirt and blood off and then moved to the far end of the row of sinks. I looked into the mirror and smiled at the growth of hair on my face. It had been almost two weeks since I had last shaved. I pulled out a can of shaving cream and my razor, but opted to keep the short beard, for now at least. I liked it.

I couldn't help but think of how bad that night had gone. Everything was routine until the group of men showed up a few blocks away from the house. People never approached us unless they meant trouble. And lately we found plenty of trouble. A quarter of our assignments in Iraq ended up with us getting into an external conflict apart from our primary target. And it always ended up being a mistake on the part of the men who engaged us. Not just our group either, this was the standard for all ops teams. The men who tried to take us on had no way of knowing who we were. And they had no chance of living long enough to find out. Despite that, they always engaged us. It was like they had nothing to live for.

Or maybe they had everything to die for.

On this night, though, those men hung back, like they were waiting for something. Maybe they were playing games with Bear, the false advancement and the tall man yelling at us. That would have been enough to throw us off, make us think that they were a group of regular guys. Of course, they could have just been a group of regular guys. Maybe they were waiting for us to do something. It'd give them a reason, at least.

Then there was Martinez. He was in rare form tonight. Bear and I worked together, but we weren't always assigned to the same CIA team. We floated between four different groups. We'd spent enough time with Martinez to know he was a high-strung, high-motor midget. His guys weren't any different, either. This incident wasn't the first time that we'd squared off. It had happened three other times, including once on base. But this time he seemed to be daring me to make a move. Every time we got into it, it was because he pushed the limits on acceptable treatment of detainees. He pushed further than ever before with the woman, and in front of her kids, nonetheless. For a moment, I thought he'd pull the trigger. He might've had I not said anything. His guys sure wouldn't stop him. Pussies.

The gauntlet would come down on me over this. I knew that. It was their word against ours. There were four of them and two of us. Their bosses wouldn't bother questioning the family for their account of what happened. My bosses were in the U.S. in the Carolinas. I needed to call Abbot and Keller. Give them my side of the story before anyone else talked to them.

I got dressed, exited the restroom and walked back down the empty hallway to our room.

I pushed the door open and called out to Bear from the hallway.

"What do you say we go grab something to eat?"

No response.

"Bear?"

I stuck my head in the room. The back door stood open. I figured he'd stepped outside for some fresh air and decided I might as well join him. I grabbed a beer and found my jacket. My hand reached inside a pocket, searching for my cell phone. Oddly, it was missing. It had been in that pocket all night long. I hadn't even taken it to check the time.

"Bear, have you seen my phone?"

Still no response.

I stopped moving things around on the table and looked toward the back door and took two steps toward it. I saw Bear standing on the back patio, and he looked at me, but he said nothing.

"Bear?"

He clenched his jaw, but did not respond.

"Jack Noble," a voice said from behind.

I stopped and turned my head and saw two men, both armed, standing in the back of the room. I knew them by face, not by name. They weren't friends of mine. I dropped my beer and clasped my hands together behind my head. I looked at the floor and saw fizzing beer wrapping around the soles of my boots.

Two other men led Bear inside. He looked at me and shook his head. Pretty obvious what he was thinking. Same thing I was.

"What's going on, guys?" I said.

"Shut up, Noble," one of them said from behind me.

"You can't just detain us without a reason," I said.

The man laughed. "We're in Iraq, Noble. We can do whatever the hell we want."

They grabbed my hands, forced them down and behind my back. I felt the thick plastic zip ties close around my wrist and draw my arms close together. The hard plastic dug into my skin the more I moved.

"If we want you to disappear," he continued, "there are thousands of miles of deserted land where we can bury you."

"That a promise?" I said.

"Keep talking." He grabbed my wrists and forced them upward. "And it will be."

"Jack," Bear said, his voice was low and trailed off at the end.

I looked at him.

He shook his head and looked down at the floor.

I followed his gaze and saw my cell phone on the floor, crushed.

"You know, I already talked to Col. Abbot about what happened tonight." I paused. "He's sending a team to investigate Martinez."

The four men laughed.

One behind me said, "You think we're worried about Abbot? He has less say here than he does in America." He walked around me, stopped with his face inches from the side of mine. "He doesn't have crap for pull with us. Our chain of command moves up a hell of a lot faster and farther than yours."

I cleared my throat but said nothing. I felt a knot form in the pit of my stomach but didn't let my external expression change.

"Are you getting this, Noble? You're screwed. Nothing is going to get you out of this."

For what, I thought. Kicking that douchebag Martinez's ass? Hell, the other ops teams we worked with all said they couldn't stand him.

"Let's go."

They led us through the front door, down the hallway, and outside to a Humvee parked in front of the building. We climbed in through the back passenger side door. Bear and I sat in the middle. Two men sat in back with us, guarding the door. They held their weapons firmly pressed into our sides.

"Make sure you avoid the potholes," I said.

Bear chuckled. The four men didn't. These guys had no sense of humor.

"Shut the hell up, Noble," the driver said.

I did.

We drove on in silence across the base. Stopped in front of the building we used for detaining persons of interest. Guess that was what Bear and I were now.

3

We waited in a gray concrete room. Mold covered the plaster ceiling and the rank smell of mildew overpowered my senses. There were no windows, only a single steel door, and just one table with two small wooden chairs. We were not in a cell, it was an interrogation room. We hadn't spent much time in this part of the building, as the CIA had specialized agents on site to handle the interrogations. Even if they used the field agents we were attached to, they wouldn't allow us in the room with a prisoner. We had been trained in interrogation techniques, though, and I had a feeling that training was about to come in handy.

Bear paced the room along the walls. "You believe this garbage?" He said it flatly, shaking his head.

I shrugged. "We knew it was coming."

"Yeah, but..." He threw his hands up and resumed pacing.

"Just sit back, nod your head and don't admit anything."

"You know I can't stand that suck up crap, Jack."

"Me either, big man, but we've got no choice. Let's just take our slap on the wrist, get out of here and get Abbot on the phone."

"Abbot," he said, shaking his head. "Who knows what they've filled his head with by now?"

I agreed. Chances were he and Keller had already been briefed and given Martinez's side of the story.

"He'll listen to us. Don't worry about that."

Abbot would listen, I felt sure of it. He had known both of us since we were eighteen years old. He oversaw our training and our placement within the agency.

"I still can't believe he agreed to these garbage orders," Bear said.

"Yeah, well," I said. "I don't think he had much choice."

Following the attacks, the agency pushed hard for all of Abbot's men to deploy to the mid-east. Most of the guys went to Afghanistan to join in the hunt for Bin Laden and the attack on the Taliban. The remaining twelve of us were sent here. The best of the best is what Abbot had said, and that meant our talents were being wasted away guarding frigging doors and doing grunt work for guys like Martinez while he and his team botched opportunity after opportunity. These guys weren't operators, they were baboons.

"What the hell are you smiling at?" Bear said.

"Didn't realize I was."

He stopped in the corner opposite the door and leaned back against the wall. "I'm done with this."

"The team?" I said.

"Yeah," he said. "I'm ready to get out."

Bear and I joined the Marines at the same time. And even though I only had a few months left until my enlistment ended, he still had two years to go. When the topic came up, neither of us could make a good argument for or against doing another two to four years. I didn't know what I would do next, though. I'd spent enough time dealing with CIA operatives that I knew I wanted nothing to do with the agency, even though I had an open invitation after my enlistment was up. The FBI wouldn't talk to us without law degrees, so they were out, not that they were ever really in. There was local law enforcement and government agencies like the DEA, but after everything I'd done, I didn't take to the idea of having to follow laws in order to do my job.

"I'm starting to feel the same way," I said.

I leaned my head back, resting it against the top of the wooden chair, studying the mold patterns on the ceiling that started in the corner near the door, spread out evenly across the ceiling and then turned to the right, stopping before it reached the opposite wall. I wondered what was above the room.

"Look, Bear—" A rap at the door interrupted me.

Bear straightened up and braced himself against the wall. His face looked tired and pale and void of any emotion. He stared down at his boots. They'd taken our laces, but left us with our shoes.

I thought about staying seated at the table, but if they decided to come in and rush us, it would be better for me to be standing. I got up and went to the far end of the room, away from the door, and leaned against the wall adjoining Bear's wall.

We heard another knock and muffled voices, and then the distinct sound of a key entering the chamber of a lock followed by the latch turning. The handle bent down and the door cracked open a few inches. The barrel of a gun pushed through. I felt my stomach sink into that all too familiar personal pit of despair.

"Turn and face the wall!" a man shouted.

Bear looked at me, his expression spoke volumes. His cheeks turned red, his nostrils flared, his wide eyes were covered by his heavy brow, furrowed down. I knew that look. Hell, I'd been on the wrong end of that look a couple times in recruit training, before we were forced on this journey together.

"Take it easy," I said.

He started toward the door.

"Bear," I said, arms out, palms facing him. "Don't do it."

He stopped, face went slack, head lowered toward the floor. He turned slowly, placed his hands against the wall.

I did the same. Part of me wanted to turn and fight, just like Bear, but I knew the best option for us was to get out of that room, off base, and back to the U.S. That wouldn't happen if we attacked the men who had the power to let us go.

The door creaked open on rusted hinges. The concrete walls absorbed the echoes of dull footsteps as several men entered the room. I turned my head to get a count.

"Face the wall, Noble."

I felt something in the middle of my back and quickly realized it wasn't a hand. It was the barrel of a gun. I turned my head toward the wall, focusing on an imaginary spot. The scuffs and cracks in the wall created an illusion of a woman with one arm over her head and the other across her belly. Maybe she was on an island somewhere. Then it hit me. I knew what I'd do instead of re-enlisting. I'd get out and head to an island where I'd open a bar and live the dream.

"Sorry to do this to you, Noble." Hot stale breath hit my neck and wrapped around my face, entering my nose despite my attempts to exhale heavily and send it away.

Men appeared on either side of me, grabbing my wrists and jerking my arms behind my back. They wrapped steel cuffs around my wrists, and I heard them click as the cuffs locked and tightened. I glanced over and saw three men attending to Bear, two on either side of him working his arms, while another man stood directly behind him, holding a gun to the back of his head with one hand, handcuffs dangling from the other.

"Let's move, Noble."

I didn't budge.

"Don't make us move you."

I said nothing and didn't move.

"We warned you."

I'm not sure what was worse. Knowing I was about to get hit over the head with a blackjack, or the blackjack actually hitting me over the head. It didn't matter. The world went black right after impact.

I'M NOT sure how long I was unconscious. I couldn't be sure I had actually regained consciousness. My head hurt like hell. The dark room offered no signs as to whether the sun had come up yet or not. I blinked the sleep away, opened my eyes and squinted as they adapted to the dark surroundings. Tainted air burned my lungs during a deep breath. They stretched and filled to capacity. The slow exhale eased some of the pressure and pain in my head.

My hands and arms tingled. I shook them until full sensation returned. Then I sat up and stretched my arms behind my back and felt a twinge of pain in my shoulder followed by a shot of pain radiating across my back and down my arm. I must have injured it when they cuffed me, although I didn't remember resisting hard enough for my shoulder to sprain. It didn't matter. I took another deep breath and pushed away the pain, closed my eyes, tried to relax. I managed three exhales and then there was a knock on the door.

"Come in," I said, not bothering to get to my feet.

The key clanked against the lock. The latch clicked. The handle turned down and a bang filled the room as the door whipped opened.

Two men entered the room. Both were tall, skinny, dressed in camouflage cargo pants and dark t-shirts. No weapons visible. I didn't recognize either of them. I found that odd. I thought after six months I'd seen every person on this base. They took a seat at the wooden table in the middle of the room.

"Sit," the dark-haired one said.

I got up slowly, using my hands to keep my balance in check. Took a couple steps and grabbed a hold of the wooden chair across the table from the men. I sat down and placed my hands on the table. They didn't appear to be armed, but that didn't mean they weren't. I didn't feel like finding out just yet.

They had two manila folders spread out in front of them. Both were open. They rifled through papers. A quick glance confirmed the files were all about me.

"You guys know what time it is?"

They said nothing, just continued to look at the papers.

"You know, most of that is fake," I said. "Fodder for the guys at the Pentagon."

Neither of them looked up. Neither of them said anything.

"What's for breakfast today?"

"Noble," the bald one said without looking up at me. "Shut up."

I smirked, sat back. *Should I push my luck? Why not?*

"I'm an egg man, personally," I said. "Pancakes hang in my gut too long.

And cereal, shoot, cereal never fills me up. But give me three or four eggs and I can go all—"

The bald man looked up from his papers. "I said quiet. We'll be with you in a moment."

"Ok," I said. "Just trying to pass the time."

His partner pushed back in his chair and stood. He put his hands on his hips and stared down at me. His head bumped the single light in the room, which hung on a fixture suspended over the table, and sent it swinging. Shadows danced around the room and across his face. His look went from menacing to evil with each pass of the light.

The bald man turned his head. "Jim, don't let him get under your skin."

Jim sat down. He appeared to be done with the files in front of him, and he fixed his gaze on me. He worked thick muscles in his jaw while rubbing his cheeks and chin with one hand.

"Jack," the bald man said. "I'm Bill, and this is Jim. We just want to ask you a few questions about last night."

"I don't remember anything," I said.

"This will be a lot easier if you cooperate, Jack," Jim said.

I shrugged and looked at the wall beyond their heads.

"Start with what happened between you and Martinez," Bill said.

"He's a great guy," I said.

"He's an asshole," Bill said. "We know that. But he says you attacked him. Do you agree with that?"

"That's what Martinez says, huh?"

They both watched me, arms in front of them, hands on the table. I'm sure they studied every subtle movement I made. I could answer one way, and these guys would know if I was lying or not based on how I shifted my eyes, twitched my nose or licked my lips. I did my best to mirror their posture and movements, which were meant to be as neutral as possible and draw no reaction.

I sat up straight and placed my hands on the table, palms down. "Martinez reached the point of using unnecessary and borderline force with members of a family who likely had no reason to be in the room."

"Likely?" Jim asked.

"Yes," I said. "Likely."

"Why do you say that?" he asked.

"You just know, Jim. Just like you guys just know."

He blinked a few times, quickly, but said nothing.

"Then what happened?" Bill asked.

"I told him to stop."

"You contradicted your team leader?" Bill said.

"He's not my leader," I said. "I'm a Marine, deployed here in support of your teams. I answer to Colonel Abbot and General Keller."

"You answer to your team—"

"Jim," Bill said, cutting his partner off. He smiled at me. "Then what happened?"

"He told one man to stay behind and then led me and my partner outside at gunpoint."

Bill looked down, scribbled something on a pad of paper, and then resumed his neutral stance.

"Go on."

I shrugged. "Then—" I paused and turned my hands up. "Then we fought."

"And the outcome?" Bill asked.

I opened my mouth to answer, but a loud knock at the door interrupted. The balance that had been restored in the room was about to be offset.

Jim pushed back in his chair, stood and walked to the door, then cracked it open an inch or two. He nodded a few times and then pulled the door open all the way. A third man entered the room. He was taller than the other two and looked like he weighed as much as both of them combined. Sweat beaded up on his waxed bald head. He stood at the end of the table, between them and me, looking down across his wide nose in my direction.

"Jack," Bill said. "This is Nathan."

I looked up and nodded. Nathan grumbled.

"You just keep answering questions like you have been and Nathan here will stay nice and quiet."

"And if I don't?"

Nathan laughed. Jim joined him.

Bill frowned. "Let's not go down that route."

The set up was familiar. I recalled studying it, role playing it during my initial training. I knew they didn't have anything on me. They knew it, too. This was all a show. The only question I had was how far they would go with the charade.

"I'm going to get right to it, Jack," Bill said. "When did you return and kill the family?"

Kill the family?

"I'm afraid," I said, "I don't know what the hell you're talking about. We didn't kill anyone."

My mind raced through the events of the night. Could he be talking about the guy we ran over? That dumbass put himself in our way while we were escaping an escalating situation.

Bill looked up at Nathan and shook his head. "Not yet." He lowered his gaze and looked at me again. "Gallo says you told him to get out. He did. Says he watched the house and that you and your partner didn't leave."

"How'd we get back here then?"

"You know what I mean, Noble." Bill's lips thinned and he crossed his arms over his chest. "You didn't leave before he left."

"Yeah, well, his team had an interest in hurting us and the family." I licked my lips and leaned forward. "If you are looking for the person or people who killed that family, you should investigate them."

"We did," Jim said. "They said before they left they heard gunshots from inside the house."

I sat back. This wasn't good. Not by a mile. Their word against ours and out here our word didn't mean squat. It didn't matter what I said in here, they wouldn't believe my story.

"I want my CO on the phone. Get me Colonel Abbot."

Bill shook his head. "It's not going to work like that, Jack." He looked up at Nathan and nodded. "We're ready for your confession."

The big man slipped past my peripheral vision. The thuds of his feet hitting the ground continued until he was behind me. If there was any doubt as to where he stood, it voided the moment he put his large hands on my shoulders. His hands slid down around my biceps, then threaded between my arms and my body, forming a knot behind my back. In an instant he jerked me out of the chair to my feet.

Jim moved to the spot where Nathan had been standing and pushed the table out of the way.

Bill stood in front of me, eye to eye. "Why'd you do it, Jack? Why'd you kill that family?"

I shook my head.

"I didn't kill anyone. You got this backwards."

"Then why is a family dead?" Jim said, pushing Bill to the side. "You go into a house, last known person inside. And now a man, woman, and two innocent children are dead."

"They were all innocent," Bill added.

My arms pulled further backward as Nathan's grip tightened. The strain against my shoulder shot pain down my arm. They'd obviously rehearsed this several times with other detainees. I had an idea what would come next.

Jim leaned in close. His eyes darted side to side as he looked into my eyes. "You have any idea how much you disgust me?"

"I got an idea."

He laughed and looked down while rubbing his chin with his left hand. He jerked to the side and his right arm swung up, his fist clenched and aimed at my head. The blow landed on the side of my face. A flash of white light filled my eye and faded as pain pulsed through me.

"Tell us what happened," Bill said.

"Nothing happened," I said. "We—"

He delivered another blow, this time to my stomach. I prepared for it by tightening my abdominal muscles. The blow didn't have the desired effect. Although, I did catch Jim shaking his hand afterward.

"We told them to leave," I continued. "Made them promise to leave."

"And now they're dead," Bill said.

"Yeah," I said. "I'm guessing they didn't heed our advice."

No one said anything.

"Look," I said. "You need to get Martinez and his guys in here. Separate them. I'm sure their stories of what transpired after they left will change."

"Thanks," Bill said. "But we don't need you to tell us how to do our jobs." He turned to Jim, nodded and stepped toward the door, his back to me.

Jim smiled, then swung twice. Both blows connected, one with my stomach, this time a bit higher and more damaging, and the other one to my face. He smiled at his handiwork and then backed up.

The second blow to my stomach had knocked the wind out of me. The burn in my lungs slowly gave way to the dull ache on my face where I'd been struck twice. I forced air through my nose and clenched my jaw while shaking my head violently.

"I can go all day," he said. "So keep up the BS."

"I got nothing to say," I said. "We didn't kill that family."

I wondered if Bear was getting the same treatment. There had been five guys in the room when they separated us. Three stayed with him, two came with me. They deemed him the greater threat because of his size. Would that translate to harsher interrogation techniques?

"Logan gave you up," Bill said.

I said nothing. I knew the line was fabrication.

"It's true. We worked him before we came in here." He turned and walked toward me and smiled. "He caved quickly. Of course, he pinned it all on you."

"Bullshit," I said. "There's nothing to pin. Bear... Logan wouldn't give in that quick even if there was."

"I'm tired of this," Bill said. He looked past my shoulder and nodded.

My arms pulled back further and I felt my body lift and then crash to the floor. Nathan had me locked up on the floor. I sat upright. His legs wrapped around me and crossed over mine. I couldn't move them.

Bill and Jim leaned over. Jim grabbed a handful of my hair, forced my head back. I felt Nathan's hot breath on my cheek. That wasn't as bad as the smell of it, though.

"What do you want?" I said, struggling to break the big man's hold on me.

"We want the truth." Bill reached behind himself and retrieved a handgun. "You either give it to us, or you die."

I closed my eyes and took a deep breath. I had their positions fixed in my head. I just needed to free one leg, so I pushed back and kicked out with my leg, only it wouldn't move. Nathan pushed down with increased force and Jim adjusted his grip on my head, gathering up even more hair in his grasp.

Bill brought the gun up and placed the cold barrel against my forehead.

The room went still with only the sounds of our breathing filling the air. I rolled my eyes back and looked up at the mold-covered ceiling.

What the hell is above this floor?

"I've got a question," I said.

Bill smiled. "Yeah? What is it?"

"You guys spray in this mold for some tactical reason? Or is it just for show?"

His smile faded and his lips thinned. He brought the gun down to my mouth.

I clenched my jaw shut tight as he tried to force the barrel past my teeth.

Jim knelt down and used his free hand to squeeze my cheeks. Bill did the same. Eventually they succeeded.

I sat there, restrained by a man bigger than Bear, with two skinny agents holding my mouth open like they were feeding some kind of wild animal. Only it wasn't a bottle of milk in my mouth.

"I'm going to give you one more chance, Noble," Bill said, his voice escalated to a yell. "Why did you kill that family?"

He removed the gun from my mouth.

"We didn't," I spit the aftertaste out, "kill anyone."

Bill nodded at Nathan and turned.

The grip on my body loosened and Nathan and Jim pulled me from the floor. Pushed me back to the wall and spun me around. They leaned in so that my cheek pressed tight against the cold concrete.

Soft thuds hit the floor behind me. Bill pressed the barrel of the gun against my head. "Sorry to do this to you, Jack."

My eyes met Jim's. He smiled, turned away.

I held my breath and waited for the shot, wondering whether my ears would register the sound of the gun firing before the bullet penetrated and shut down my brain.

And then every muscle in my body tightened at the banging that cut through the air.

4

"Christ," Bill exhaled loudly and grabbed the back of his head. "Let him go. Put the table back."

Nathan and Jim let go of me. I turned, pressed my back to the wall and inched toward the far corner of the room. The two men slid the table to the middle of the room. Bill stood in front of the door, his head turned.

The three men nodded at each other.

Bill cracked the door.

"Yeah?"

The voice responded low and hushed. I couldn't make out the words. Bill covered most of the door with his body. Nathan hung back in the corner nearest me. Jim stood a few feet from Bill.

Bill took a step back, looked over his shoulder at me and shook his head. "Nathan, watch him for a minute."

"OK," Nathan said.

Bill and Jim stepped out. The door closed behind them. Nathan walked backward to the door. He kept his eyes on me.

"Bet I could take you down," I said.

Nathan laughed. "They let you Jarheads smoke some good stuff, huh?"

I gave him a half smile and winked. "Ten seconds, fifteen tops."

His smile faded. Eyes narrowed. "Screw you, Noble. You wouldn't stand a chance."

I took a step forward. I held my shoulders back and my arms out to the side and back, ready to attack.

Nathan banged on the door.

The door clanked open and Jim stuck his head in.

"What?"

Nathan nodded in my direction. "He's getting flighty."

Jim disappeared. The door stayed open. Nathan didn't move. I had hoped my actions would get him out of the room so I could have a few minutes to check the table. No such luck. Jim and Bill returned.

Bill looked at me. He shook his head. "You must give one hell of a reach around, Noble." He pulled out a pair of steel handcuffs. Stepped toward me, slowly, his eyes fixed on mine. "You're being sent back to the States."

The left side of my mouth lifted into a smile. I held my hands out in front of me. I kept my eyes fixed on his.

"On whose orders?"

Bill didn't respond. He grabbed my right wrist with his left hand, slapped the one side of the handcuffs over my arm, lifted and tightened and then did the same to my left wrist. He took a step back, lifted his head and looked me in the eye again. "Keller."

I nodded. Keller or Abbot, it didn't matter. The decision came down from both of them. I was sure of that.

"You're not out of this garbage yet, Noble. They're taking over the investigation, that's all."

He turned, pointed at Nathan with a nod and stepped out of the room. Jim followed.

Nathan walked toward me. "Think you can take me down in ten seconds now?" He chuckled.

"Faster," I said. "I got a weapon now." I held my arms up and let the chain between the cuffs sag in a u-shape.

"You're something else, Noble," he said. "Too bad we never got the chance to work together."

He placed a large hand in the middle of my back and pushed me toward the door.

I didn't resist. What about Bear, though? I didn't want to turn their attention to him, but I had to know if he was getting out or if he was stuck here. It seemed like they had it out for me. Bear was just unlucky enough to be my partner, which was usually the case. I stepped through the doorway into the dimly lit hallway and saw Bear standing in the middle, surrounded by three CIA agents. He nodded with a wink. It looked like we were going home together.

WE PILED INTO A SAND-COLORED HUMVEE. Bear and I had the row behind the driver to ourselves. They removed the cuffs from our wrists before slamming the doors shut. The rest of the talk inside the interrogation room was just that, talk. We were free. Abbot and Keller weren't going to investigate this anymore than I would. Worst case, we'd be reassigned to Afghanistan. At least there we could do some good. Maybe they would keep us in the States and assign us to a new team.

I leaned over and looked between the front seats. Two men I didn't recognize occupied the front of the Humvee.

"Where are we going?"

Neither man responded.

I lifted my eyes and stared at the driver in the rearview mirror. His eyes, set behind puffy cheeks, didn't move to meet mine. I sighed, turned to Bear. "Where you think they're taking us?"

"They said home," he said.

"You believe that?"

He shrugged and let out a loud exhale. "Think they're just going to take us out to the desert and leave us?"

"Thought's crossed my mind." I wiped sweat from my brow. "Although, I don't see them leaving us there alive," I added.

Bear laughed. "These guys can't take us."

The driver looked up and met my stare in the rearview mirror. I smiled and winked as I watched to see what kind of reaction Bear had gotten with his remarks.

The driver shook his head. "We're not leaving you in the middle of the desert. Just sit back and relax. You'll be on a plane soon enough."

"Back to the States?" I asked.

The driver shook his head. "No clue, man. I'm just driving you."

I looked at Bear and shrugged.

"They tell you about the family?"

"Yeah." Bear paused while rubbing his beard. "You think it was Martinez?"

"Makes sense. I showed him up. He had itchy fingers to begin with."

"Pretty brazen of him, if he did."

"Yeah. Maybe he figured he could pin it on us and get away with it." I stared at the tattered canvas ceiling. "You know you're going to have to shave that beard when we get back on base."

"You too, Jack. You too."

I nodded and scratched at the growth of hair on my face. Leaned back in my seat and closed my eyes. The only thing I could think of was getting the hell out of Iraq. Back home. It didn't matter where. Any place in the U.S. would be fine with me. My thoughts slowed and I drifted off to sleep.

The car jerked to a stop. I woke up, opened my eyes. The side of my face ached from the cheap shots in the interrogation room. I saw Bear sit up straight and yawn. He'd fallen asleep too. He cocked his head, side to side. His neck popped and he grunted.

I turned my head to look out the window. We were parked next to what looked like a single landing strip tucked between hills of sand on all four sides. At one end sat a small commuter jet.

"We're here," the driver said.

"No shit, Sherlock," I said.

"Get out of my ride," he said.

"Gladly."

I opened the door and slid out.

Bear appeared from behind the Humvee and took position next to me.

The Humvee roared into gear and drove away. We stood alone in the empty parking lot with nowhere to run to if things got out of hand. And lately, if there was one thing you could count on, it was things getting out of hand.

Four men waited next to the plane, all dressed in khaki cargo pants, plain t-shirts, and tan windbreakers. They had holsters strapped to their thighs. Two of them held assault rifles.

One stepped forward and motioned for us to come over.

I looked at Bear. He shrugged. We didn't have any other options. If they were going to kill us, it would be now. And if that was the case, I'd just as soon get it over with. We crossed the narrow strip of gravel to the area next to the plane.

The man continued forward and met us halfway and introduced himself as Colwell. He had short brown hair and brown eyes.

"We'll be taking you to Germany, Frankfurt International," Colwell said. "Pulled some strings. You'll bypass the terminal and customs. You'll be escorted onto a flight that will take you back to the U.S."

"Where to?" I asked.

Colwell shrugged and held out his arms. "My job is to get you to Germany." He turned and extended one arm out toward the plane. "Let's get on board and get out of here."

I passed the other men without making eye contact. I had no interest in getting to know them, and I was sure they felt the same way about me. I climbed the stairs into the small jet and made my way to the back. Found a seat and collapsed into it. I closed my eyes for a second and massaged the area around my cheek. When I opened my eyes Colwell stood in front of me.

"Up front."

"Screw you. I'm not moving."

He pulled his pistol from the thigh holster. The gun dangled at his side. "Jack, move."

I sighed and stood up. "I'm unarmed," I said, holding my arms up as I passed him. His dark eyes met mine and his lips thinned. His head followed me. I could tell he didn't like being that close to me in a confined space.

"Don't care," he said. "I know all about you, Noble." He nodded toward Bear. "Him too."

"Yeah, well," I said, "I don't know jack about you."

"And we're going to keep it that way," Colwell said. "Don't want you showing up at my door one night."

"No," I looked back over my shoulder, "you don't."

Colwell said nothing.

I took my seat. Bear sat down across the aisle. He smiled and shook his head.

Ten minutes of silence passed before they taxied the plane in a tight circle. Then the small plane barreled down the runway, cut through the air and turned to the northwest, toward Germany.

I SLEPT through most of the flight and woke up as the plane descended through the dark sky toward the city of Frankfurt. Lights from cars and buildings lit up the black ground like pins poked in dark construction paper and held over a lamp. I pried my eyes from the window and looked at Bear. He clutched his seat belt tight. Only thing I found that set the big man on edge was flying. Not so much the flying part, though. He hated landing.

He glanced over at me. Sweat covered his forehead. Beads rolled down his cheek and settled into his whiskers.

"Take it easy," I said.

He nodded and took a deep breath. His shoulders heaved up and down, forward and back. I'd seen him do this ritual several times. He clenched and loosened his muscles while taking deep breaths. The series of exercises helped him overcome and tame the panic that flooded his mind. It's how we were trained to handle any situation where our mind got the better of us. No shame in feeling afraid or panicked. *Improvise, adapt and overcome.* The unofficial mantra of the Marine Corps. It always stuck with us, even if we spent the majority of our time with the CIA.

Bear exhaled, and the tension left his body. He smiled, let go of his belt and leaned back in his seat. I didn't think it appropriate to mention he'd have to go through this one more time before our ordeal ended.

The plane lurched and tires squealed as they touched down on the runway furthest from the terminal. I bounced in my seat a few times while the plane set down. The pilot brought the jet to a near stop, and then guided us along the outside track, toward a row of terminals. The plane stopped.

Colwell stood, passed by me and went in the cabin. A few minutes later he came back out and motioned for us to stand.

We did.

He opened the door and dropped the narrow set of stairs attached to the plane.

I stepped through first. A cold breeze stung my face and exposed arms. We weren't prepared for this weather. I hurried down the stairs. An idling truck waited for us near the front of the plane.

Bear came down the stairs with Colwell right behind him.

Colwell pointed toward the truck. "That's your escort to the international flight back to the States."

I nodded and waited for Colwell to join us. He didn't.

The passenger door opened. A man stepped out. He looked to be mid-thirties and wore a dark suit, red tie. He walked around the back of the truck, pulled down the gate and then turned to us. "Get in." He pointed to the bed of the truck.

I looked at Bear and rolled my eyes. He climbed up on the gate and took a seat on the wheel well, and I followed.

The man in the suit nodded at Colwell, returned to the front of the truck and sat down in the cab.

Colwell gave me a mock salute.

I gave him a middle finger salute.

He smiled.

"Friggin' cold," Bear said loudly over the rush of the wind and the truck's engine.

I didn't have to agree. My hot breath hit the chilled air and turned into a cloud of mist that rose above my head.

The truck rolled slowly on the asphalt, close to the cluster of white and gray buildings. Floodlights spaced every thirty feet lit the ground in an evenly spaced bright-dark-bright pattern. Planes were parked to the left, on the other side of a wide median filled with dead, brown grass. The truck slowed and turned toward the planes where a strip of road cut through the landscaping. We slipped out of range of the floodlights, and the sky turned dark again. I looked up, waiting for my eyes to adjust. The truck stopped before they did.

The suit stepped out of the cab.

"Get out," he said.

We did.

"Follow me," he said.

We followed him past two planes and stopped in front of a third. He held up his hand. "Wait here." He continued on a few more feet, pulled out a cell phone and made a call. After a few moments, a door on the side of the plane just behind the cockpit cracked open. Light flooded to the ground from the opening. A man dropped a rope ladder.

Our escort walked to the ladder, stopped and turned to us. "Come on, we need to hurry."

I jogged to the side of the plane and climbed up the ladder, ready to get out of the cold. The man at the top grabbed me under my elbow and pulled me up. Bear followed and our escort came up last.

"Your lucky day." The suit pointed to the blue curtain, slightly pulled back. "First class."

"You flying with us?" I said.

He nodded, put his hand on my shoulder and pushed me toward the curtain.

I stepped through and walked to the front of the plane. "What's your name?"

"Where do you think you're going, Noble?"

I turned, held out my arms. "Taking a seat."

"Back here." He pointed at three seats in the middle of the aisle, last row in first class. "You sit in the middle. I'm on that end," he pointed across the row. "Big man right here," he patted his hand on the back of the end seat nearest us. "My partner will stay right there, across the row from him."

"You know," I said, taking my seat, "I'm more dangerous than him."

"I don't doubt that one bit, Noble."

"What's your name?" I asked again.

"McMurray," he said. "You can call him Otto." He pointed at his older partner, who hadn't said a word the whole time.

Otto looked up from his newspaper and nodded. His deep-set dark eyes revealed nothing. He brushed his silver hair back and returned to reading.

"What are the chances we can get some coffee?" I said.

Otto laughed. "Stewardess." He tapped his fingers on his blue rubber armrest and waited a beat. "Guess you're out of luck. They'll board the plane in half an hour or so. Try then."

We barely talked the rest of the night. I fell asleep before we reached the Atlantic Ocean and woke up over Georgia. Bear started his relaxation exercises when the pilot announced we were making our final descent to Atlanta's Hartsfield-Jackson Airport. A few minutes later we were on the ground.

The stewardess announced first class could depart first. Bear and I stood. Otto remained seated. McMurray stood.

"You guys get off here," McMurray said.

"You're not escorting us any further?"

"I was told to get you to the U.S. You're someone else's problem now."

I shrugged. Followed Bear off the plane. We walked down the jetway. I expected to find an armed escort when we stepped into the gate. It was empty. We made our way past the mostly empty seating area and headed toward the center of the terminal, where the escalators to the tram were located. Aside from a few early passengers, the terminal was barren. I checked my watch. Not even four a.m. yet. Another hour and the place would be packed with early morning travelers.

"Coffee." Bear pointed toward one of the only open stores in a section between gates.

I followed him over, ordered a black coffee and a cream cheese Danish, and then paid for both of our orders. After the girl handed me my change, I stepped further down the counter where I found a lid and grabbed a handful of napkins. I snapped the lid on the cup and lifted it to my face. The hot steam escaping from the lid burned my upper lip and outer edges of my nose. I inhaled anyway. The heat faded, giving way to the full, dark aroma of the coffee and its promise of caffeinated energy.

Hard and loud footsteps echoed behind me. *Click-clack.* They stopped a few feet away.

"Jack Noble. Riley Logan. Don't move a damn muscle."

5

"CHRIST," BEAR SAID UNDER HIS BREATH.

I turned my head toward him. My eyes followed the speckled countertop then lifted to meet his. He shook his head, straightened his back and lifted his hands over his head.

I looked over my shoulder. Two men dressed in jeans and button up shirts stood ten feet back and aimed their handguns at us.

"I said don't move a damn muscle," one said. "Eyes forward. Arms up."

I reluctantly placed my coffee, of which I still hadn't had a sip, on the counter, and then I raised my hands.

The lady behind the counter stood motionless, mouth open, arms held out to her side. Our eyes met. A tear rolled down her ebony cheek. I gave her a halfhearted smile. She looked away.

Two men closed in from the side. They were dressed the same as their partners. They approached us slowly and cautiously, guns drawn.

"Nice and easy," one said as he approached me from behind. "One arm behind your back."

I lowered my arm. He grabbed it.

"Now the other," he said.

I did as he said.

Cold steel gripped my wrist and pinched my skin as the handcuffs tightened and locked.

"Do we really have to go through this?" I said.

"Shut up, Noble," one of them said.

I dropped my head and considered the odds. It was two versus four. Not so fair after all, for them at least. A hand at my back guided me to the side. I turned my head and watched three of the men converge on Bear while the fourth kept a gun aimed at me.

Bear cooperated by bringing one arm down, then the other. They cuffed him, turned him and led him toward me, one man on either side of him, their hands gripping his elbows.

One of them stepped forward. He had brown hair and a square jaw. He holstered his weapon. "This is going to go nice and easy, guys." He pointed down the terminal. "To the escalator, board the train, get off. Don't make eye contact with anyone. Don't talk to anyone. Don't talk at all. Got it?"

I nodded. Didn't look to see if Bear did or not.

He continued. "At Arrivals turn right toward the North Terminal. Continue past the baggage claim and head outside. A van will be waiting for us."

I wondered why he talked to us like equals instead of prisoners.

"If something happens, and we get separated, you meet us at the van," he said. "If we find you anywhere other than the van or on your way there, we have orders to shoot to kill." He paused, his eyes batting between the two of us. "Can I trust you guys for a few minutes?"

"Yeah," I said.

He nodded at one of the others, who then removed our handcuffs. "Let's go."

We followed him through the terminal, down the escalator and into the train. We sat in the back. They stood in front of us. The train stopped at terminal A. We all exited and followed the signs to the escalators that led to the empty Arrivals gate. It seemed that nobody had any loved ones arriving that early, or maybe they just didn't care at four a.m. We passed the baggage claim and walked through two sets of tinted automatic doors, coming to a stop outside.

The air felt cool and refreshing. Orange light flooded the sidewalk and six-lane divided road between the building and the parking garage. A dark van with tinted windows idled nearby.

One of the men pointed and went over to it and opened the back door. He gestured toward us, and Bear and I followed and got inside.

"Middle row," he said.

We sat in the middle. I didn't recognize the driver. He must have been waiting in the van the whole time. One of the men joined him up front, in the passenger seat. The other three sat in the row behind us. The van pulled away from the curb, followed the curved airport road and merged into the early morning traffic heading northbound on I-85.

HALF WAY through Atlanta we merged onto I-20, heading east. After leaving the city, the drive felt long and pointless. Our escorts didn't talk. We had no idea who they were. No names, ranks, or affiliations were given. Although, I had a feeling these guys were CIA.

When I tried to talk to Bear, it was met with a command to shut up. I resigned myself to staring out the window at the redundant scenery.

Darkness faded, and the gray clouds gave way to the rising sun. The sun painted the sky shades of orange and red. The sight held me captive for half an hour.

I leaned forward and stuck my head between the driver and passenger seat. "Where are we going?"

The man in the passenger seat turned his head to look at me and said nothing.

I sighed, sat back.

We reached Florence, SC around nine a.m. I asked if we could stop for breakfast. We didn't. Instead, we merged onto I-95 northbound. I hoped that meant we were heading to Camp Lejeune. I feared it meant we were heading to Langley, which would be bad.

Our CIA command was held deep below the Air Force base. We'd be under their command down there.

Camp Lejeune was located on the coast of North Carolina. It was home to several Commands, including the Marines Special Operations

Command, and was often used for amphibious assault training. Camp Lejeune also served as our unofficial command under Colonel Abbot. We weren't stationed there, though. We weren't stationed anywhere. However, we did have to report quarterly if we weren't on an extended deployment.

I leaned forward again, looking at the driver and then the passenger.

"Where're we going?"

The man in the passenger seat turned his head. "Lejeune."

"That's where we were heading, anyway. You guys saved us the cost of a rental."

He turned away. Said nothing.

I sat back and took a deep breath. Only one thing bothered me.

"Lejeune," I said to Bear.

"Yeah," he said then paused for a moment. "Brig's there."

That's what bothered me. The Marine Corps Brig was located there, and it was capable of housing up to 280 inmates.

FOUR HOURS later the van rolled past a red brick sign that read, "CAMP LEJEUNE: HOME OF EXPEDITIONARY FORCES IN READINESS," and stopped in front of the base's main gate. The man in the passenger seat stepped out of the van then opened the side door. Two of the men in the back seat got out. They ordered us out and walked us to the corrugated steel guardrail that surrounded the guard house in the middle of the road.

We stepped over knee-high guardrails. A baby-faced MP waited for us. He nodded to our escorts and they turned and got back in the van.

"Move to the front," the MP said. He pointed past the red stop sign and extended red and white gate crossing the road. "They'll be up to get you soon."

We moved to the other side of the building. I leaned back against the brick exterior and stared down the deserted tree-lined street that led to the main base. Things hadn't changed much since the last time we were here. That was six months ago. Just before our deployment to Iraq.

Bear leaned over. "This garbage stinks." He kicked one leg up, placing his heel against the brick wall behind us. "Abbot should have met us out here."

"I thought he would," I said. "He's the reason we're here, though, and not the island."

"Think he knows we're here right now?"

"I hope so, Bear. I honestly do."

A dark sedan approached from the base, slowed down and made a U-turn in front of the guard station and stopped in the middle of the road, and then both front doors opened.

"Turn around," an MP said as he emerged from the passenger side. "Hands on the wall."

I turned to Bear, rolled my eyes, then continued around to face the wall.

The MPs were on us a few seconds later. They were cautious and calm. They didn't shout or use force with us.

"Just a formality," one of them said. "Nice and easy. Let's get this over with."

I didn't resist when they pulled my arms down behind me and handcuffed me. Neither did Bear. A few minutes later we were in the backseat of their cruiser.

"Take us to Colonel Abbot," I said.

The driver looked up and made eye contact with me in the rearview mirror. "He's not here."

My heart sank. Abbot was our only contact on base.

"Know where he is?"

The driver shook his head.

"I'll need to get in touch with General Keller then."

"You realize you're detained, don't you?" the other MP said.

I exhaled and shrugged.

"Just take it easy. You guys will be settled in soon."

I kept hope up that they were taking us to the barracks and putting us up for the night. But the further we drove, the more I knew that wasn't going to happen. The car finally stopped in front of the brig. The MPs got out. The back doors swung open.

"What are we being held for?" I asked.

"Not our concern," the MP said while pulling me out of the car by my elbow.

I pulled back.

"Let's not go down that route. OK, Noble?"

I eased up, swung my legs out of the vehicle and planted my feet on the ground. The MP pulled me up and dragged me over to where Bear and his MP escort waited by a door that led inside the brig.

"Let's go," the MP said.

He led me through the door into the building. We walked down a wide, dimly lit industrial gray hallway past several administrative offices. Signs next to each door indicated a name or division. We passed through two sets of security doors then stopped in a cold square room, painted white with a foot wide gray stripe about four feet off the ground. A pale, skinny MP stood behind a counter at the far end of the room. He looked me up and down, did the same to Bear, then disappeared from sight.

"Strip," one of the MPs said. "We'll worry about your hair and beards tomorrow."

Bear and I removed our clothes.

The skinny MP reappeared a few minutes later and handed us a pair of green sweat pants and a gray shirt, slippers for our feet, and some toiletry items. We quickly dressed and gathered up the other items. The MPs led us out of the room, down a darker and narrower hall and through one more set of security doors. We entered one of the housing areas. They split us up, leading Bear up a set of stairs and me down a set.

It was quiet, eerily so. The air was sterile and smelled of disinfectant. The place was everything you would expect a Marine prison to be.

We stopped in front of a cell. The wall was solid except for a small hole cut in the middle of the door. I held my breath in anticipation.

"Don't move." The MP let go of my arm and unlocked the cell door. Opened it and turned to me. "Go in."

I stepped through and heard the door close behind me. The walls of the room were painted gray and a single light fixture was fixed in the middle of the ceiling. A toilet and sink sat in the back left corner. In the middle of the room was a small table with two permanently attached chairs. A small window in the middle of the back wall allowed sunlight to flood into the room. On the other side of the room, next to the window, sat a metal bunk bed. The top bunk was empty. A man with a shaved head lay on the bottom bunk, ankles crossed, one hand behind his head, the other on his bare stomach. A colored tattoo of a phoenix covered his hairless chest. His eyes shifted from the crossbars of the top bunk to me.

"Who're you?"

"Noble."

"Never heard of you."

"That's the way I like it."

"What're you in for?"

"Murder. You?"

He shrugged.

"How'd you get to keep all that crap on your face?"

I scratched at my short beard. "It bother you?"

He swung his feet over the side of the bed, planted them on the floor and stood. He was about the same height as me with a similar build.

"Yeah, it bothers me."

"It won't for long," I said. "They're shaving me tomorrow."

"How bout I take care of it now?"

I held my ground, prepared for him to attack. Turned out, I didn't have to wait long.

He took a step and reached out with a wide right hook intended for my face.

I ducked the blow and exploded upward, driving my right fist into his jaw. A crack confirmed that I had either broken or dislocated his jaw, perhaps both.

He hit the ground like a bag of sand and his head smacked against the concrete floor with a thud.

I waited a few seconds to see if he'd regain consciousness. He didn't. I picked him up and dumped him on his mattress, positioning him the way I found him. Then I walked over to the door, stuck my face dead square in the center, which was open to the outside except for four iron bars.

"That all you got?" I yelled through the hole.

6

THE ADRENALINE WORE OFF, AND I DOZED OFF, MANAGING TO SLEEP THE REST of the afternoon. I awoke to the sound of my cellmate moaning. I opened my eyes. It took a few minutes to remember where I was and why. I looked around the cell. The reddish orange light of the setting sun filled the room. I swung my head over the side of the bunk and looked at the injured man below me.

His eyes darted to mine. He held his hand to his jaw. Guttural sounds formed in his throat as he tried to speak. His wide eyes teared over.

"Shut the hell up unless you want the other side broken too," I said.

He fell back onto his pillow, looked away and said nothing.

I continued to stare at him, driving the point home. The cell became quiet again.

A knock on the cell door broke the silence. Someone shouted something through the hole in the middle of the door, then a key clanked into the lock. The door swung open and an MP entered carrying trays of food. He stopped when he caught sight of the man on the bottom bunk.

"Jesus Christ," the MP said. "What the frig happened to him?"

"He slipped," I said, "and hit his chin on the sink."

The MP put the trays on the table then clicked a radio on his upper chest fixed to his shirt. "I need medical in echo wing, first floor, cell four." He fixed his brown eyes on me. "Tell me what happened. The truth."

I sat up. "I told you already. He fell and hit his chin on the sink." I leaned over the side of the bed and looked at my cellmate. "Ain't that right?"

He grunted then moaned.

I smiled.

"Yeah, well, we'll figure this out," the MP said.

"You do that," I said.

"Why don't you get down and stand in that corner for now." He pointed toward the toilet and sink.

I swung my legs over the side and hopped down and moved slowly to the corner of the room without taking my eyes off the MP.

He didn't take his off of me, either, keeping his palm rested on the handle of his tear gas gun.

I sat down on the stainless steel toilet and placed my hands on my knees. The MP seemed jumpy, and I didn't want to give him a reason to gas me.

Two medics followed by two more MPs entered the cell a few minutes later. The medics attended to the injured man on the bottom bunk while the MPs focused their weapons on me.

"Jaw's broke," one of them said. "Bruised to hell on the left side."

The MPs looked at me.

"He fell," I said.

The short medic left the cell then returned a moment later with a wheelchair. They helped the man off the bed and into the chair and wheeled him out of the room. I found myself alone with the three MPs.

One closed the door and leaned back against it. His wide frame blocked the hole in the middle of the door. The other two approached me and boxed me into the corner. Their names were affixed to their uniforms, Bates and Sanders.

Bates spoke first. "Like to beat up on our prisoners?"

I didn't respond.

Sanders reached down and grabbed my shirt and pulled up on the collar, presumably trying to lift me to my feet.

I didn't move.

"Get up," he said.

I didn't.

"Now," he said.

I still didn't.

They both reached down and pulled me from the toilet and slammed me against the back wall. I turned my head and caught a glimpse of the final sliver of the orange sun before it set behind the expanse of trees that ringed the brig.

The MPs jammed their elbows into my chest as they leaned into me, taking turns punching me in the stomach, making sure to avoid my ribs. I kept my abdominal muscles tight as long as I could. Eventually the blows wore me down and they landed successive shots that knocked the wind out of me.

They backed off, and I slid to the floor. I clutched and dragged my nails across the concrete in an effort to get to my knees and fill my lungs with air. The edge of my vision darkened. Finally, my lungs expanded and air rushed in through my mouth. I gasped and exhaled several times.

"We'll be back for you later, Noble," one said.

The last one left the cell, and the door slammed shut. I knelt on the floor until the sick feeling in my stomach subsided. Then I pulled myself off the ground and checked the trays on the table. Chicken, green beans, bread and lukewarm coffee. I hadn't eaten in nearly a day and it had been at least that long since my last cup of coffee. It ended up being one of the best meals I'd ever had.

There wasn't much to do in the cell, and the nap combined with the attack by the MPs left me too amped up to sleep. I paced the space between the bed and the table, walking from the door to the back window. Stopped and stared out the window. A few lights flickered in the distance. Other than that it was dark and quiet and serene.

A bang at the door jarred me back to reality and I spun around with my arms held in a defensive position. The door opened, just a crack.

"Noble," a voice called.

"Yeah," I said.

The door opened further and General Keller stepped in, stopping just inside the entrance. His close cut grey hair gave way to a face that looked like it was cut from steel. There were deep lines etched into his forehead, thinner lines spread out from the corner of his blue eyes and from the sides of his mouth.

I nodded at the man and felt relief wash over me.

He smiled, looked to the ground then back up at me. "Christ, Jack, what did you get yourself into?"

"We didn't do anything."

Keller looked over his shoulder. "Leave us."

"Sir, that man physically injured his cellmate earlier. It's not safe for you—"

"Dammit, I said leave us. Do you want me to kick your ass, Corporal?"

"No, sir."

"Then get the hell outta here."

The MP disappeared from sight, and the cell door shut and remained unlocked.

I cast a glance toward the door.

"Don't think about trying to run, Jack," Keller said. "Not now, at least."

"OK," I said.

"And what is this mess all over your face? And your hair?" He shook his head. "I remember when you were a clean cut kid. Now you look like... like one of those bums my daughter used to bring home."

"With all due respect, General," I said, "I've seen your daughter. Do you think she'd be interested in me with my present look?"

Keller tried to look stern, but gave up and laughed. "Sit the hell down, Jack."

I sat across from him and waited for him to continue.

"I don't know where this is coming from," he said. "But I'm having a bitch of a time getting you two out of here. Did you piss anyone off over there?"

"Other than Martinez?" Jack said. "Not that I can think of."

Keller nodded. "Someone is issuing this order." He looked over his shoulder, then back at me. "I talked to someone, someone up high, who admits you had nothing to do with the murder of that family. Off the record, of course."

"Of course," I said. "You think it's the CIA then?"

"It'd have to be, wouldn't it?" he said. "Who here would do this? I run the damn show and it's not me. There's no one between us."

I nodded. "Have you spoken to Abbot?"

"Yeah. Haven't been able to talk to him about it yet. But I'll keep trying. I'm not as connected as I used to be, Jack. That's what everyone says, at least." Keller stood. Reached into his pocket then threw a pack of cigarettes on the table. "You keep those, Jack. Maybe you can trade them for something."

I thanked him and rose. He stuck out his hand, palm facing me, indicating I should stay where I was.

"I'm working on getting you out of here. Stay alert, you got it?"

"Yes, sir."

———

THE LIGHT in the cell cut off at ten p.m. The lights outside the cell dimmed and didn't provide much illumination through the square hole in the door. I climbed into my bunk and tried to get some sleep. It didn't happen. My face hurt. I tossed and turned most of the night, replaying the events of the past forty-eight hours, trying to figure out how I got from Baghdad to Camp Lejeune, from a free man on a mission, to an imprisoned soldier.

Every fifteen minutes a patrol passed the door. I'd hear them approach with deliberate steps on the walkway. They'd reach the door, stop and look in. The room would darken for five seconds, and then the patrol would back up and move to the next cell. I thought about getting up, standing at the back of the room, to see what they'd do. In the end I stayed in bed.

I dozed off a couple times, each time the sleep lasted longer than the last. By six a.m. I was fast asleep when banging erupted against the door, waking me up.

I sat up, shaking the sleep away.

The door swung open and two MPs entered the cell while a third remained firmly planted in the doorway, his taser aimed in my direction.

"What's going on, guys?" I said.

"You should've been up an hour ago, Noble. Get the hell out of bed."

They pulled me down and dragged me out of the cell and down the hall.

"Where are you taking me?"

They pushed and pulled me along and said nothing.

Prisoners hanging out on the walk parted to the side and ducked into open cells to make way for us.

We stopped outside the head. One MP opened the door, and the other two pushed me inside. All the showers were running, and the room was steamy. A group of four men stepped through the cloud of warm mist and walked toward me. They wore the same uniform as every person who wasn't an MP, and had to have been the four biggest guys in the place.

I looked back over my shoulder. Two of the MPs had followed me in and now blocked the only way out. I assumed the third was positioned on the other side of the door, blocking the only way in.

The largest of the men walked up to me. He had to be six-five, maybe six-six, and had forty to fifty pounds on me. He licked his lips and grabbed my shirt and leaned in close. I mentally flinched at the smell of his hot, foul breath as it washed over my face and invaded my nasal passage.

"You like attacking my friends?" he said.

I shrugged. "Depends."

His lips curled as he grinned, revealing two missing front teeth, one up top, one on the bottom. As fast as his smile faded, he brought his forehead down into mine.

Tears flooded my eyes, and I felt a rush of blood flow through my nose and trickle down across my lips. I spun around and reached out for the wall so I could brace myself and get my bearings. I found the wall, steadied myself and blinked away the tears. My eyes refocused, and I saw the four inmates forming a semicircle around me.

"Guys, look," I said. "We don't have to do this."

The big man laughed.

I swung my foot as hard and fast as I could in the direction of his crotch. It connected with a thud. He dropped to the floor, a huddled mass gasping in pain. I twisted sideways and drove my elbow into the nearest man's face. Blood sprayed from his nose upon impact, a crunching sound preceded his scream. I blocked a punch by the third man and countered with a shot to his neck, just above the sternum and just below his Adam's apple in the soft fleshy spot that offers little to no protection. His eyes bugged out and his face went pale, then turned a light shade of blue while he gasped for air.

The fourth man landed a blow on the side of my face. I wasn't expecting it and the force of it spun me. I regained my footing and charged him as he lunged at me. We met somewhere in the middle where a grappling match ensued. We rolled on the floor, fighting for position. I ended up on my back where he managed to get his arms wrapped around my neck in a choke hold. I arched my back and squeezed an arm between his, loosening his grip.

I caught sight of the MPs. They were leaning back against the wall, laughing at the action.

I scanned the room and spotted the big man on his knees, trying to get to his feet. The other two prisoners posed no immediate threat.

My legs climbed their way up the man I was wrestling with until I managed to get my shin across the front of his neck. A quick shift of momentum and I spun around, coming out on top with his neck in a death grip between my legs. I arched and twisted. His mouth opened and his face turned pale and his neck was close to snapping. He slapped and clawed at my legs. I felt like a savage, yelling as I neared the moment when I planned to lurch and end his life.

The MPs intervened, one hitting me over the head with a blackjack. They pulled at my legs and freed the man from the death grip. His loud gasps for air filled the room as he crawled across the slick floor on his belly to the row of sinks.

I felt my body pulled from the floor and flung through the air and pinned against the wall. The MPs held me there while three of the four men stood.

The door opened and the third MP stuck his head in. "What the hell is taking so long?"

No one said anything.

He entered the room.

"Jesus Christ," he said. "What the hell happened in here?"

I caught his eye and smiled. "You guys got no idea who you're messing with, do you?"

"Shut up."

The MP with the blackjack slammed it across my stomach.

I grimaced against the pain, forcing a smile even though I couldn't breathe.

"Just end him, and let's get out of here," the third MP said.

The big man stepped forward. "Let me do it." He bared his teeth at me.

"No," the MP said. He grabbed the big man by his shoulder. "You guys need to get the hell out of here."

The big man spun. "Like hell, man. He's ours." His large arm stretched out toward me. He took two steps forward, looked back at the MP. "Just try and stop me."

I knew the MP wouldn't, so I did. I lifted my leg toward my chest and drove my heel down and into the side of his knee. Popping sounds filled the room as his ACL and MCL tore upon impact. He went down hard, his head slamming into the tile floor, a pool of blood forming under him.

All hell broke loose after that.

The MPs quickly took care of the two standing prisoners, restraining them and piling them near the door. Easy work, considering I'd already beaten them. With the prisoners out of the way, the MPs turned their attention to me. I stepped forward and was met with a quick strike to the side of my head by the blackjack. Searing pain traveled from the spot of impact, and then around my head. The impact knocked me off my feet. I landed hard on my side. The MPs pulled me off the floor. Two of them pinned me against the wall. They leaned in with all their weight to hold me still. The third took the blackjack and placed it across my throat. He leaned on it in an effort to force my windpipe to close shut. My oxygen-starved lungs screamed out in pain. The edge of my vision darkened while flashes of light filled the center. The last thing I remembered before passing out was the sound of the door opening and a deep voice yelling my name.

7

A HARD SLAP ACROSS MY CHEEK JARRED ME FROM MY UNCONSCIOUS STATE. I opened my eyes. Bear stood over me. His eyebrows pushed down over his eyes. He helped me to my feet and steadied me against the wall. I tensed and checked over the room. Empty. Trails of blood led from the middle of the floor to the door.

"What the hell happened, Jack?"

I shook my head. "They wanted to cut my hair."

"What?"

"Retaliation," I said. "For breaking my cellmate's jaw."

"Yeah, I heard about that."

"He swung at me first."

Bear took a step back. His lips thinned as he looked me over. "Christ, they did a number on you. How do you feel? Can you walk?"

I pushed away from the wall. Took a step, steadied myself.

"Yeah, I think I'm good."

I walked to the row of sinks and looked at my reflection in the mirror. Blood trickled from a small gash on the side of my head. My nose was red and swollen, but not broken. That was the worst of it, though. There were no broken bones and no major lacerations. I came out of it OK, all things considered.

"Where'd everyone go?" I said

"They scattered when I came in." Bear said.

"How'd you know?"

Bear hiked his shoulders. "Word spread pretty quick down there," he nodded toward the door, "that they were fixing to do a number on you." He shook his head. "Damn, they sure did. We've got to get out of here, Jack."

"It's not that bad." I ran cold water over my face, grabbed a handful of paper towels and cleaned out the cut on the side of my head. It'd probably needed stitches, but it'd heal without them, leaving a scar behind, of course. Scars were good for my line of work, though. They added an element of intimidation.

"I'm with you, Bear. Lead the way, and I'll follow."

At that moment the door swung open and a middle-aged man dressed in his combat utility uniform stepped in. He looked around the room, his gaze stopping at spots where a struggle had obviously occurred. His eyes set on Bear, then shifted to me. He shook his head.

"What a mess," he said.

I looked at Bear. He nodded at me. We both moved to the center of the room, within arm's reach of each other.

The man took a step forward, letting the door swing shut behind him. He pushed his arms out in front of him. "I'm a friend."

We said nothing.

"Abbot sent me. I'm Lt. Col. McDuffie."

"Sent you for what?" I trusted nobody at this point.

"To get you guys the hell out of my brig," he said. "Look, this is a mess. I don't like it. I don't know where it's coming from, and I don't like it."

His eyes bounced between me, Bear and the bloody mess in the bathroom. He turned, opened the door and stuck an arm out. When he turned around again, he was holding fresh clothes. He tossed a shirt and a pair of pants to Bear.

"Noble, why don't you get cleaned up first," he said, clutching the clothes intended for me.

I nodded, headed to the back of the room and showered. The hot water stung as it washed over cuts and scrapes. I grimaced against the pain and hurried to finish. Then I put on the fresh clothing, which consisted of camouflage cargo pants and a plain gray t-shirt.

"I've got boots for you guys in the car," he said.

"The car?" Bear asked.

"Yeah, the car," he replied with a hint of annoyance in his voice. "I told you I'm getting you out of here." McDuffie turned and opened the door and stopped and looked over his shoulder. "The MPs outside this door are mine. They won't do anything to you if you stick with me. They'll follow us and keep you safe."

We followed him out of the head without any further questions, heading toward the stairs. We took one flight up and then passed through a security door. We followed the narrow hall to the check-in room where McDuffie retrieved our belongings from the pale skinny MP at the counter. I wondered if anyone else ever manned it, or if Lance Corporal Skinny was the only one. We left the room and continued on, through the wider hall, past the two sets of security doors and all the administrative offices.

I had to shield my eyes from the sunlight when we stepped outside. As my eyes adjusted, I caught sight of a platoon doing their morning PT jogging by. Their rhythmic pace matched their cadence:

I know a girl dressed in Red,
Makes her living in a bed.
I know a girl dressed in black,
makes her living on her back.
I know a girl dressed in green,
and she is nothing but a screwing machine.
Ooooorah up the hill, Ooooorah down the hill

McDuffie walked around the front of a black Ford Crown Victoria parked against the curb ten feet away. He turned to us. "Get in the back."

Bear shifted on his feet and hesitated. He glanced at me, looking for confirmation that it was OK to get in the car.

I felt the same hesitation. At this point we only had McDuffie's word. Neither of us knew the man, and Keller hadn't mentioned him when he visited me the night before. There was the very real possibility that this could be a set up, and both of us knew it. We felt it, instinctively. But in the end, I decided I'd rather take my chances in the car with the middle-aged Lt. Col., than with the prisoners and MPs in the brig.

"Go on," the MP behind me said with a push to my back.

"Let's go, Bear," I said.

Bear opened the back door on the passenger side and got in the car.

I walked around the back of the vehicle and grabbed the handle, but stopped before getting in.

McDuffie stood with his hand on the open door to the driver's seat. He studied me for a moment. "Go on, get in."

"I can trust you, Lt. Col.?" I said.

"I'm on your side, Jack," he said.

WE LEFT CAMP LEJEUNE BEHIND. Houses, fields and stretches of forest passed by in a blur. We drove for forty-five minutes without saying a word.

McDuffie pulled into the parking lot of a small shopping center near I-95, just outside of Fayetteville. He parked the car and opened his door. "Let's grab something to eat." He pointed toward a 24-hour breakfast diner.

We got out and crossed the parking lot. McDuffie walked in front, and Bear and I followed close behind.

We must have missed the breakfast rush because the diner was empty. A cute hostess warily greeted us and sat us in a booth then dropped off a carafe of coffee. Moments later a blonde-haired waitress with red lipstick and a name tag that read Jenny took our order.

Bear and I sat shoulder to shoulder, across from McDuffie. He said nothing to us. His eyes scanned the road in front of the diner. He pulled out a pack of cigarettes, lit one and dropped the pack on the table.

I followed his gaze, stared out the window, watched cars pass by on the road we had traveled on.

"Glad you guys could make it," a voice said from behind.

I turned and saw Abbot standing there, dressed in faded blue jeans, a white polo and a tan jacket.

"Sorry things got out of hand in there, Jack," he said.

I hiked my shoulders. "Not your fault."

"You should have never been in there."

"Hear anything?"

He shook his head. McDuffie slid in toward the window and Abbot sat down next to him.

"No," Abbot said. "I've called every contact I have." He placed his elbows on the table and steepled his fingers. "Half of the bastards wouldn't even take my call."

"What about General Keller?" I asked. "Did he reach out to you?"

"Briefly," Abbot replied. "After he spoke with you." He grabbed a menu, looked it over, then poured himself a cup of coffee from the steaming carafe. "He's looking into it, too," he added.

"So what now?" Bear asked.

Abbot held the mug to his mouth and blew into it, sending ripples through the coffee and a puff of steam into the air in front of him. He took a sip and his mouth contorted in response to the aftertaste. He set the mug down then lowered his hand to his lap, returning a moment later with a set of keys that he tossed onto the table.

"D.C."

"Washington?" Bear asked.

"Yeah," Abbot replied. "Neil Delaney."

He slid a folded piece of paper across the table toward me. I reached out, grabbed it and then unfolded the paper, reading the name and phone number on it. I offered it to Bear, but he shook his head, perhaps because he trusted me with the information, or maybe because he didn't want to take his eyes off the men who sat across from us.

"Who's that?" I asked.

Abbot cleared his throat and fidgeted with his scuffed gold wedding band. He brought his hands to his face and rubbed his chin with the tips of his thumbs, holding his index fingers inches from his mouth. His eyes shifted toward the window and he said nothing.

"Colonel—"

Abbot raised his hand and shook his head slightly. "He's an old friend.

He's got contacts that I don't. Delaney might not have any idea what's going on when you meet with him, but give him a few hours and he'll be able to tell you everything. Who's behind it, why they're behind it, how high it goes. Everything, Jack."

He glanced over my shoulder and lifted an eyebrow while nodding once.

The waitress stopped next to me, a brown tray perched on her hand and shoulder. She expertly balanced it while setting our plates down in front of us, muttering each order under breath. In a thick, East Carolina accent she asked, "Can I get y'all anything else?"

We shook our heads in unison and waited for her to leave before speaking.

"What else?" I asked.

Abbot looked up at me with his mouth slightly open like he wanted to say something else but was holding back.

"I know there's something else, Abbot. What is it?"

He placed his fork and knife on the edge of his plate, sat back in the booth, folded his hands together and placed them on the table. He stared at me for what felt like ages before finally speaking.

"There's the chance, Jack, that this could be coming down his chain of command. Understand?"

"You haven't spoken to Delaney," I said, not a question.

"No, I haven't. So you need to know," he lifted his hand and wagged an outstretched finger between me and Bear, "that this could go badly. Once he digs into it, if it's his, uh, organization behind it, he'll turn. He's that kind of guy. Personal loyalties are superseded by the job."

I nodded. I understood, in a sense. In another I didn't. The job was just a job. There was a personal code of conduct that couldn't be violated. You might be able to move the line now and then, but there had to be a point where the line couldn't stretch any further without breaking. And when a friend needed help, that line was drawn thick and deep.

"Who does Neil work for?" Bear asked.

Abbot shook his head and looked down at his plate.

Bear looked from him to McDuffie. "You know?"

McDuffie hiked his shoulders and shook his head. "Never heard of him in my life. I'm a damn prison warden. I'll leave the spy stuff to you guys." He chuckled and then stuffed his mouth with a forkful of butter and syrup-covered pancakes.

"That information is on a need to know basis," Abbot said. "Right now—"

"Don't tell us we don't need to know," I said. "At least give us this."

Abbot said nothing. He crossed his arms over his chest and turned his head toward the window.

I sighed and shook my head. "OK, then. How're we getting up there? Can't travel on a plane right now. TSA will flag us."

Abbot turned his head, pointed at the keys. "You're taking my car."

I reached out, picked the keys up off the table and stuck them in my pocket.

"But listen," Abbot said. "It won't be long before that car's hot. Understand? Like I said, I don't know who is watching and who's not."

I nodded.

"You see blue lights, you be ready to run, Jack."

I nodded again.

We finished breakfast without saying another word, and then we walked out together. Bear and I collected our things from McDuffie's car. Abbot walked us to his.

"Delaney," Abbot said to me. "He's a bit of a shifty character, Jack. But you can trust him."

"As long as his agency isn't behind this," I added.

Abbot pursed his lips together and drew his eyebrows down. "Yeah."

We stopped in front of Abbot's car, a new silver Audi A8. I whistled and ran my finger along the sleek body of the car. "So this is what my dirty work pays for, eh?"

He stood behind the car and smiled while I opened the driver's door and slid into the leather bucket seat. He moved forward and rapped on the window. I started the car and rolled the window down.

"Take it easy with her," he said. "Please. Oh, and no smoking."

I shrugged. "We'll see."

"Here," he said. I looked over and saw him holding a billfold stuffed with cash and a few credit cards. "This should cover anything you need. Pin numbers are in the center. Commit them to memory. There's a bag in the trunk, where the spare would normally be. Inside that bag is an assortment of weapons." He paused and stared at me for a moment. "Don't get caught with them."

By the time I had the money in my pocket, Abbot was gone. I turned the key in the ignition. The engine roared approvingly. We pulled out of the parking lot and then hit the I-95 north on-ramp. I pushed the gas pedal and hit 85 miles per hour before we merged onto the interstate, then wove the car through traffic and into the fast lane.

Bear was the first to speak. "What's your read on this?"

I thought for a moment. "Abbot's not going to BS us."

"You still trust him?"

"He got us out of the brig." I glanced over at Bear. He rubbed at his beard. "If he wanted us out of the way, what better place than in there?"

I kept my eyes on the line of cars, SUVs and minivans in front of me. A mental inventory of license plates piled up and nothing seemed out of the ordinary. I held my breath as we passed a parked state trooper and let my foot off the gas. I kept my eyes fixed on him in the rearview mirror. He didn't move. I felt a release of tension for the first time that morning.

"What about this Delaney guy?" Bear asked.

"We'll have to get a read on him quick," I said.

That much was true. We'd know within a few minutes if Delaney was friend or foe. A public meeting would be necessary.

"Make sure we meet him somewhere with a lot of witnesses," Bear said.

"Reading my mind again?"

He laughed. "Guess I've known you too long." The big man yawned, leaned back. "Think it's time I get a new partner. You're getting too boring."

I smiled and looked up at the rearview mirror. "Yeah, well you think this mess we're in is boring?" I nodded toward the back of the car at the set of blue lights that closed the distance in a few seconds. The state trooper pulled his cruiser within a few feet of our rear bumper. The lane to the right was open, but he wasn't passing. He must have clocked me going twenty over the speed limit. Or worse, Abbot could have reported the car stolen. Would he do that so quickly?

I cursed under my breath and moved into the right lane. The cruiser pulled over the same time I did. I hit the brakes and dropped the speed to fifty-five. Then I pulled onto the shoulder, prepared to stop. My mind raced thinking of the next set of actions I'd need to take.

Instead of following us onto the shoulder, the cruiser passed by.

Bear let out a loud sigh. "Thought we were goners."

8

THE DRIVE TO D.C. TOOK JUST UNDER SIX HOURS. WE TOOK I-95 PAST THE outer loop to I-395. Crossed the Potomac and drove into downtown. I found a parking garage near the National Mall on 11th Street. We left the car there and exited the garage, turning left toward Pennsylvania Avenue.

I pointed at a store across the road. "We stand out. Let's get some clothes."

I found a brown leather jacket, t-shirt, and a pair of jeans. Bear donned a sweatshirt and cargo pants. We paid for the clothes and left the store.

"Grab some lunch?" Bear pointed at a pizza place across the street.

I pulled out the paper Abbot gave me with Neil Delaney's number written on it.

"Yeah, let's eat, and then I'll call our contact."

We sat at a table on the front patio. A black gate stretched out and separated the open air dining area from the sidewalk. Pedestrians walked by with their heads tilted back, noses in the air, taking in the smell of fresh baked pizza. A waitress with straight brown hair and very little makeup came to our table. We ordered a large cheese pizza and two beers. The air was cool and the smell of melted cheese, rising crust, and tomato sauce overwhelmed my senses. It felt like a perfect day. It would be a perfect day if it weren't for the fact we were trying to save our lives.

Tourists, business people, and even politicians passed by. "Look," Bear said. "Robert Marlowe. Seen him on the news a lot over the last year. Deputy Secretary of Defense."

I watched the group of men approach. Marlowe walked in between two other men. He wore a blue suit, red striped tie, and a tan London Fog overcoat. His hair was a mix of silver and black, thin on top. He was clean shaven and wore thin glasses. He was tall and looked to be in good shape for a man his age. The men on either side were approximately the same age. I figured them to be politicians as well. Two Department of Defense agents followed close behind. They were younger than the three politicians and wore dark suits, dark glasses, and earpieces, just like you see in the movies. They scanned the street and sidewalk. I figured time moved in slow motion for them. They were trained to notice everything and take out a threat at a moment's notice.

"Wonder if he knows about us?" I said.

Bear smiled. "I could go ask."

"Find out if he'd never heard about our program. Can you imagine what that investigation would uncover if he hadn't?"

"Don't want to," Bear said shaking his head. He took a bite of thick crust, chewed on it for a moment, and then swallowed. "From what I gather," he wiped his face with a napkin, "this guy is big on Iraq, us getting involved over there. So who knows, maybe he does know about us. Maybe he's the reason we're there."

I watched the Deputy Secretary walk past us without batting an eye in our direction. One of the agents assigned to Marlowe appeared to take notice of me watching him. The agents gaze lingered on me longer than anyone or anything else he'd looked at. I glanced away, reaching into my inside coat pocket in an effort to give him something to think about. A moment later I looked up. They had kept walking and were fifty feet past our position. It looked like the agent had forgotten all about me. I knew looks could be deceiving, though.

The waitress dropped the bill on our table. I finished my beer and set the empty bottle on top of two twenty dollar bills so the breeze wouldn't blow them away. We exited the patio, and joined the stream of people walking toward the National Mall. We turned right on Pennsylvania Avenue and crossed the road at 15th Street, near the White House. I cut through the grassy area between 15th Street and the Presidential Park to get away from the crowds. Groups of trees were spaced out along the lawn, offering shade from the bright sun above.

I stopped near a fountain, looking around to make sure no one was within ear shot. Once I was sure the area was reasonably secure, I reached into my pocket, pulled out my cell phone and the paper with Delaney's number. My fingers punched the numbers on the keypad. I brought the phone to my head and heard the call connect.

A man answered on the third ring. "Yeah?"

"Yeah, is this Neil Delaney?"

"Who's this?"

"You don't know me, but we have a friend in common."

I looked over my shoulder and saw a couple walking hand in hand in my direction. I turned to the right and walked toward a tree.

"Who? Who's the friend?"

"Colonel Abbot," I said.

Delaney said nothing.

I looked around again, as if he were standing nearby. "You there?"

"How do you know Abbot?"

"He's my CO."

Delaney cleared his throat and continued in a hushed voice. "This isn't a safe conversation to have on the phone." He paused. "People are — uh, you know where the Lincoln Memorial is?"

"Yeah," I said. "I can find it."

"OK, you do that. Meet me there in forty-five minutes. Got it? Can you get there by then?"

"Yeah, sure."

"Stand on Abe's right side, fifth step from the top. Got it?"

"Right side facing him or his right side?"

Delaney sighed. "Facing. I got to go. Forty-five minutes. Be there. You got one shot."

"What do you mean one—" The call disconnected before I could finish.

I shook my head, and tried not to read too much into Delaney's behavior. It was possible I caught him off guard and that's why he acted the way he did. I pushed away from the tree and started walking toward the park, on the lookout for Bear.

He found me first.

"How'd it go?"

I put the phone back in my pocket and turned to face him. "He knew something, that much was obvious." I looked past Bear, trying to figure out where he had been during the call. "The moment I said Abbot was my CO, Delaney freaked."

Bear leaned his head back, looked up at the tree in bloom. "What do you mean, freaked?"

"Went silent. Started whispering."

"Guess this won't be a wasted trip then, will it."

"We have to be at the Lincoln Memorial, forty-five minutes. Right side, fifth step from the top. He'll find us."

Bear pointed toward the Washington National Monument. "That's at the far end, past the monument there."

"Guess we should head over then."

IT TOOK twenty minutes to reach the Lincoln Memorial, which meant we had twenty some odd minutes to hang back. This was a great place for people watching. Didn't matter who they were, the Lincoln Memorial, of all places, had the ability to have a profound effect on its visitors.

I checked my watch and saw it was about time. "Let's go." We walked up three sets of stairs, staying to the right and stopped on the fifth step to the top. I leaned back against the handrail. An older woman gave me a look for blocking the railing, so I stepped to the side and let her pass.

"Wonder what this guy looks like," Bear said.

"Look for a suit."

"That's about twenty percent of the crowd."

"He'll find us. Relax."

"Like hell I will. You don't know who he might bring with him."

"Not by his tone, Bear."

Bear said nothing.

I scanned the incoming crowd looking for the mental image I had of the man I had spoken with on the phone forty minutes ago. A few people had the look, but weren't quite right. Then I spotted him.

"There," I said, my arm outstretched pointing to the base of the stairs. He stuck out like a sore thumb among all the tourists. And being that it was past lunchtime, a Fed this close to the memorial just didn't make sense.

"Who?"

"Silver and brown hair, a little thin on top, glasses. Kind of mousy looking, but in pretty good shape for his age."

"Got him," Bear said. "Tell you what," he looked back at me, "I'm going to hang back a bit. OK?"

"Good idea."

I kept my eyes focused on the middle-aged man ascending the steps. He reached the middle of the longer stretch of sand-colored stairs and looked up in my direction. He scanned the area and fixed his stare on me. He gave me a slight nod as he came to a stop.

I nodded back and checked the area around him, looking for any sign of a threat. I assumed he did the same.

He started in my direction again. He stopped two steps below me. He looked past me, said, "Neil Delaney."

I grabbed his hand and shook it. "Noble."

He nodded. "I've heard of you."

"I can't imagine that's a good thing."

He pursed his lips and shook his head.

"Big man back there is Bear. Riley Logan."

Delaney looked over my shoulder and acknowledged Bear. Then he held out his arm and said, "Let's move to the back."

We walked up the remaining stairs, turned right and took a path that led us behind four huge columns, stopping behind the fourth. There, we huddled close together.

"Any place less public we can go?" I asked.

Delaney shook his head. "This is the best place. For now." He looked over his shoulder. "Less chance something will go down here. Got it?"

"Yeah," I said. Paused and then added, "I got it."

"So you two are part of the operation, huh?"

I leaned back against the thick column, crossed my arms over my chest and nodded. "What do you know about it?"

Delaney hiked his shoulders, cocked his head. "A bit. CIA sponsored. They take Marines out of basic—"

"Recruit training," Bear interrupted.

"Yeah," Delaney said. "Whatever. Take fresh *recruits*," he looked at Bear and paused a second, "and then put them through their spec ops training. Turns you into well-rounded operators that they can blame crap on when someone else screws up. You're crazy enough for the job, 'cause let's face it, you wouldn't have enlisted in the Marines unless you were crazy to begin with." He smiled and batted his eyes between us.

We didn't smile back.

"Yeah, well, anyway, so they get you before you're done. Before you've been completely brainwashed into that bullshit *oorah* culture. That was one of their initial design flaws. The first group to come through had been through basic, uh, recruit training and A school. They were Marines and it caused problems when you had a dick of a spec ops team leader. They scrapped the first wave. You guys were part of the next bunch. They hit the jackpot with you two and the others that came through around the same time. From 95 through early 2001 you pretty much handled domestic stuff that the CIA couldn't legally touch," he waved his hand in a semi-circle for emphasis, "and occasionally a friendly nation. You always traveled two by four, two of you, four of them. You spent some time in South America. Colombia, if I'm not mistaken?"

I nodded. He had done his research, or was more involved in this than Abbot let on.

He continued. "Then the attacks happened and you were re-prioritized. Almost all of you were shifted from here and friendlies to the Middle East. I'd say eighty percent of you guys went to Afghanistan chasing Bin Laden and the Taliban. But not you, though. You're in Iraq, right?"

I nodded again.

"So over there you're—"

"Look," I said. "I appreciate the history lesson, but we got a situation going on here. Someone is setting us up and we don't know who. We go through Abbot and Keller in the Marines and then to the CIA. It's not Abbot. It's not Keller. So it must be someone in the CIA. Can you help?"

He took a deep breath, held it a moment and then exhaled loudly, letting his lips flap as his puffed-out cheeks decompressed like a tire after a blowout. "I can't say much more than I have. Not here."

"Who are you with?" I said.

Delaney flashed a crooked smile as he held out his arms and shrugged.

"You're not CIA, not the way you referred to the program being sponsored. Definitely not FBI. We wouldn't be talking to you if you were."

Delaney chuckled and shook his head vigorously.

I continued. "NSA?"

He continued shaking his head. "No, Jack. Not CIA, FBI, or NSA. Look, who I'm with isn't important. The information I have is what's important."

"Then let's have it."

"Not here, Jack. I guarantee you they are out there, watching us right now. They've probably been watching every move you've made since leaving Camp Lejeune."

I fought the urge to look around. It appeared Bear was doing the same. I saw him cast his stare toward the ground.

"Give me an idea of what it is then," I said.

"I'm not quite sure what it is. Well, I wasn't sure. I think I know now. What I can tell you is there is some shady stuff going on, guys. Very shady. I have some documents for you." He paused. "I didn't know what I was looking at until today. Not till your call. You mentioned Abbot and everything came to me. I uncovered this stuff not too long ago. But it didn't make sense. Got it?"

"No," I said. "I don't *got it.*"

"It's going to make sense tonight." He took a few steps backward. "Wait for my call. Tonight, Jack. I'll bring the documents you need."

I watched him go down the stairs, then cut diagonally across the mall and disappear out of sight.

"Ready to go?" Bear asked.

"Nah," I said. "Let's wait a few. Find a good tourist group to assimilate into."

Bear laughed loudly. "I'm six-six, you're six-two. We don't assimilate anywhere we go, Jack."

9

DELANEY CALLED SHORTLY AFTER SIX P.M. HE TOLD US TO MEET HIM AT NINE that night at a park in McLean, Virginia. At eight o'clock we went to the garage, got in the Audi, and left downtown DC. Took I-495 heading west and got off at the Georgetown Pike. Grabbed a bite to eat at a fast food joint then headed west. The entrance to Scotts Run Nature Preserve was less than a mile from the interstate. I parked the car in the deserted parking lot, choosing a spot close to the access road that led in and out of the park. I rolled my window down and cut the engine.

We sat in silence for ten minutes, looking and listening. The empty parking lot indicated all visitors had left before we arrived. The sound of an occasional car passed from the Georgetown Pike behind us. We were hidden from view. That worried me. We would be out of sight if this was a setup or if we had been followed.

"I don't like this, Jack," Bear said, right on cue.

I leaned forward and nodded. Checked the side mirrors. "I'm about fifty-fifty on it."

Bear pulled out a cell phone and flipped it open.

"Keep that covered." I pointed at the bright square of light the small screen emanated.

A twig snapped from behind the car. Both of us froze. My eyes darted to the rearview mirror, looking for the perpetrator. I saw nothing but darkness and the faint outline of trees and bushes. I placed my hand on the door handle and slowly cracked the door. I stepped out of the car, my body hunched over. I clutched my Beretta in my hand and walked to the back of the vehicle. Behind me, a light on a utility pole turned on with an electrical buzzing sound and faint orange light flooded the area. I stood five feet from the potential assailant. Our eyes met and locked. He sat down, scratched behind his ear with his rear paw and then took off into the woods between the parking lot and the Georgetown Pike.

Bear had stepped out of the car just before the dog took off. He laughed and shook his head.

"Damn, if we ain't on edge."

On edge didn't begin to describe how I felt at that moment. Considering everything we had been through and adding in the lack of sleep, I found myself surprised that I hadn't taken poor Fido out. That would have been bad. I don't think I would have ever been able to forgive myself if I shot a dog.

I returned to the car and placed my hand on the ignition. The orange light from above lit up the inside of the car.

"Don't like sitting out here under these lights."

Before I could start the car, my cell phone rang and I answered without looking at the display.

"Where you at, Delaney?" I scanned the small strip of grass at the edge of the parking lot that separated asphalt and trees.

"About one hundred yards in." He spoke quickly and in a hushed tone.

"From where?"

"Go to the northwest corner of the parking lot and walk straight north."

I covered the phone and looked at Bear. "He wants us to walk in there, blind."

Bear shook his head.

"No deal, Delaney," I said. "The parking lot is lit up. We'll be sitting ducks crossing it. You come out here."

His heavy breaths filled the ear piece of my phone.

"You there?" I said.

"Yeah," he said. "I'll meet you at the edge of the lot. Drive over."

"Delaney," I said and then paused an extra second. "If this is a setup, so help me, I'll end you first."

I flipped the phone shut and started the Audi and drove as close to the shadows in the middle of the lot as I could. Parked in a spot where two circles of orange light couldn't quite reach. I cut the engine and sat motionless for a minute.

After a pause, Bear whispered, "You see anything?"

I shook my head. Picked up my phone and dialed the last number that called me.

"I see you," Delaney said.

"I don't see you," I said.

I heard rustling mixed in with his heavy breathing. "OK, I'm," he paused to take a deep breath, "right in front of you."

I strained to see past the orange glow that hovered over the strip of grass in front of the woods. The effect left the space between the trees darker than the night sky. I looked at Bear and nodded.

"We're coming over."

I hung up the phone, stuffed it in my pocket and slowly opened the car door. "High alert, Bear." I turned my head as I said it and saw that Bear already had his gun drawn and held out in front of him, ready to go. We scanned the area as we walked. My pulse quickened with every step. The woods were so close, yet so far away, and there was plenty of time for a trained sniper to take both of us out.

"Here," Delaney called.

I caught sight of his pale hand waving in between two pine trees. I gave him a quick "cut it" signal and changed course to his direction. A moment later we slipped behind the tree line. I nodded at Delaney and kept walking.

"Where are you going?"

"Further in," I said.

I walked without light and without knowing where I was going. It didn't matter. We just needed to be out of sight of the parking lot should someone pull up and aim a floodlight in our direction.

Delaney followed behind, complaining. "Stop. C'mon, Noble, this is far enough."

I ignored him and kept walking with Bear beside me keeping pace.

"No, no, no," Delaney said.

I looked over my shoulder and saw him leaning against a tree.

"I know where this is going," he said. "I keep following you and I'm a dead man. Right?"

I stormed up to him. "Turn around."

He didn't.

I grabbed him by his jacket and forced him around. "You see that," I stretched one arm past his face, toward the parking lot. "See those orange lights?"

"Uh, yeah, I see them."

"OK," I said. "Now imagine a car pulls up. Shines some powerful lights into the woods. If we can see those lights, then they will sure as hell be able to see us."

"What about night vision, Jack?"

"We blend."

His head bobbed up and down, slow and steady. I assumed that meant he understood and I began walking again.

"Just a bit further," I said. "Now, come on."

We walked in silence for a few more minutes, changed direction and came to a clearing in the woods. The moon provided enough light for us to see each other clearly. I checked over my shoulder to make sure the lights of the parking lot were out of sight.

"What do you have for us, Delaney?" I said. "What did you bring us out here for?" I leaned in close enough that he could see the look on my face, even in the dark. "It better be damn good, too," I added.

He reached into his coat pocket.

I drew my Beretta and pointed it at his head.

"Relax," he said pulling his arms out slowly, a key dangling from a carbineer clip held tight between his thumb and forefinger.

"What's this?" I said.

"A key to a locker."

"What's in the locker?"

"The documents you need."

"Documents I need for what?"

"That will be answered when you see the documents."

"Don't screw with me, Delaney."

"I'm not, Noble. Everything you need to clear your name and take down who's behind this is in that locker. I couldn't risk bringing it out here. Bringing it anywhere with me. I had them bring it—"

"Wait, them who?"

"Don't worry about that. What's important is the location of the locker."

For some reason he waited until I asked the obvious question. "OK, Delaney, where's this locker at?"

"It's at the—"

A single shot ripped through the air and slammed into Delaney's head with a thud. A cloud of blood rose above him. His eyes rolled back and he fell to the ground, limp and lifeless.

Two more shots rang out. One hit the tree behind me, just above my head. Splintered wood and bark rained down and fell to the ground with a sound like playing cards being shuffled.

Another shot was fired, this time hitting Bear in the shoulder. The bullet hit with a thud and turned the big man sideways. He staggered a few feet then fell to the ground.

"Bear," I said, dropping to the ground. I crawled toward him. "You OK?"

He groaned and clutched at his right shoulder. He cursed out loud then said, "They got me."

"Keep pressure on it." I took cover behind a tree. I saw the explosion created by the last bullet and had a bead on the attacker's position. "I'll be right back."

I aimed my gun in the direction of the shooter and started firing until I had emptied the clip and replaced it. The sound of the shots echoed in my head. I fought against it and listened. I heard a voice calling out, getting further away. A different voice called back. There were at least two of them, and if I had to place a wager, I'd say they had night vision goggles on.

I followed in the direction of the voices, making sure to use every tree I passed as cover. I heard a voice and fired in that direction. They were running now, not caring if I heard and tracked them. They ran to the west. The parking lot was south. They hadn't come in after us. They had been here the whole time. Were we double-crossed?

I followed as fast as my legs would carry me. The moonlight penetrated through spring buds just enough for me to navigate past obstacles. A car's engine roared to life. The faint glow of red taillights became visible through the thinning trees. The car jerked forward and sped off. I fired three rounds, managing to shatter the rear window.

My lungs burned with each cold breath I took. I placed my shaking hands on my knees and bent over, catching my breath. I turned and started back through the woods. The path wasn't clear but I knew I hadn't run more than a half-mile, if that. I kept a quick and steady pace and five minutes in I started calling for Bear.

"Jack," Bear's voice rumbled in the distance.

I turned toward the sound and picked up my pace. "Keep yelling," I shouted into the cool breeze. Bear yelling was a risk, but if I didn't find him soon he might bleed out. I still had no idea about the severity of the gunshot wound.

Two minutes later I found the clearing. Delaney's lifeless body lay twisted on the ground. His legs sideways and sort of stacked one on top of the other. His torso belly-down. His face turned to the side, the moon reflecting off his dull and lifeless eyes.

Bear had managed to move to a tree and leaned back against it. Best place to be. He could adjust and take cover from a gunshot at any angle.

"You all right?" I asked.

He breathed heavily and clutched at his wounded shoulder.

"Yeah, I'll live."

"Can you walk?"

He grimaced as he pushed back into the tree and dragged his large legs under him. Slowly he pushed his body up. "Let's go."

"I could have helped." I started toward the parking lot. "I want to take a look at that when we get to the car."

"I'll be all right."

"Like hell," I said. "I'm not going to have you bleed out in Abbot's car."

The walk back to the parking lot took longer than the walk out to the clearing. Bear moved in spurts, stopping to catch his breath every so often. Fifteen minutes after we set out, we came to the edge of the tree line. Orange street lights lit up the lot. I took cover behind a tree and scanned the lot. Could they have circled back and hid out, waiting for us? There would be only one way to find out. The car was a good hundred feet away. We hid behind the dark veil of the woods.

"I'm going to jump in and start the car," I said, "then back up and pull up parallel."

Bear nodded. Said nothing.

"I'll pop open the back door," I continued. "As soon as you see that, duck and run. Dive into the back seat. I'm going to tear out of here like a bat outta hell. OK?"

He nodded again.

"Here goes," I said. "Wish me luck."

I unlocked the doors and started the car with the remote then paused. I watched the trees across the lot for any movement, but didn't see anyone or anything. I ran to the car, opened the door and got in. I watched the mirrors for a minute. The area remained still. I threw the car in reverse, backed out and pulled up parallel to the trees then leaned back between the driver and passenger seat and opened the rear passenger door.

Bear emerged from the woods, huddled as low to the ground as he could, his left arm still clutching his right shoulder. He dove head first, crashing onto the seat and pulling his legs in.

"Go, Jack."

I put the Audi in gear and sped off, making a U-turn in the lot and speeding toward the road leading out to Georgetown Pike. Halfway down the road I saw them.

They parked along the side of the access road. They stood outside the car, using its heft to shield them. They drew their weapons and aimed at the Audi.

"Brace yourself," I said.

I hit the gas and swerved to the side, sideswiping their car with the passenger side of the Audi. If luck was on my side, the driver's side door would be damaged and they'd be unable to open it. Luck might just have been on my side. The men dove away from the car and the road moments before the crash.

Bear grunted from the backseat. I raised my hand and pounded on the roof, letting out a yell.

I reached the end of the road and turned left onto Georgetown Pike without stopping. I gunned the Audi, hitting close to one hundred miles per hour. The three quarters of a mile to I-495 went by in twenty seconds. Before taking the on-ramp onto the highway, I checked my rearview mirror and didn't see any headlights approaching from behind. Either they hadn't made it to the end of the road yet, or they turned the wrong way, or they were chasing me without their headlights on. My gut told me they were chasing without headlights.

I raced down I-495 doing close to one-twenty. The Audi rode as smooth as it did when it cruised at eighty. I took the second exit and pulled into a residential neighborhood and turned on a couple of random streets until I found a cul-de-sac with two empty lots and two houses under construction. I swung the car around and backed up, leaving the car facing toward the road.

"Christ, Jack. Think I have a concussion now."

I laughed as I leaned across the front seat and fished through the glove compartment box for a flashlight. I stepped out and turned the flashlight on and coerced Bear into moving his hand away from his shoulder. The wound was deep, but clean.

"Doesn't look like it got any further than the muscle. Rotate your arm?"

Bear grimaced as he lifted his right arm and twisted it. "Yeah, nothing's broken."

"We need to get that taken care of. Tonight."

"We can't go to the hospital, Jack. Feds'll be on us in a heartbeat."

"Yeah, I know." I looked up at the clear sky. The lights from D.C. drowned out the sky to the northeast, but above us, the moon shone bright and strong and beyond its white ring of light, stars dotted the sky. The cool night air washed over my face, stinging the cuts and scrapes I received while running blindly through the woods. "I need to clean these up, too." I ran a hand across my face.

"What are we going to do then?"

I hesitated. "I know a place."

"Where?"

"I think." I paused a beat. "I think that it's best you don't know until we're close."

10

I DROVE WITHOUT STOPPING FOR CLOSE TO THREE HOURS. THE CLOCK ON THE dashboard said the time was after twelve in the morning. We crossed into the city limits of Charlottesville, Virginia. Shopping centers with empty parking lots lined the main road through town. Cars huddled around late night restaurants and bars. Neon signs announced their presence.

I pulled into a twenty-four hour gas station and stopped the car next to an outward facing pump. I placed the gas nozzle into the Audi's fuel tank and clicked the handle to auto pump. I walked inside the convenience store, grabbed a four pack of water bottles out of the fridge and filled a 20 ounce cup with fresh coffee. Hunger pains attacked my stomach, so I milled about a few minutes looking for something to eat, ultimately finding nothing. I stepped up to the counter where a freckle-faced teenager with red hair and a name tag that read "Stan" waited behind the register. He asked me how I was doing without bothering to look at me.

He grabbed the water bottles and scanned them. Looked at the coffee and punched a couple keys on his register. He looked up at me with a nervous tick of his head that threw his hair to the side and out of his eyes.

"That all?"

"Gas at pump three."

He looked at his display. "It's not finished pumping yet."

"Guess we're waiting then."

He rolled his eyes and looked away, adding a sharp click of his tongue to further express his annoyance. He walked away, pretending to attend to something else, anything to avoid dealing with people, I supposed.

I leaned back against the counter and looked around the store, taking note of all the security cameras. There seemed to be an overabundance of them.

"Have a lot of trouble with robberies here?" I said.

"Huh?" he said.

"The cameras." I pointed to the four cameras positioned throughout the store, mounted to the ceiling.

"Nah, maybe just college kids stealing stuff."

I nodded slowly. Time dragged. "Gas done yet?"

He walked back over, looked at his screen. "Yeah. Total's forty-three fifty."

I handed him three twenties and waited for my change.

I stepped out into the cool night air, put the coffee and water in the car and scanned the parking lot. There was a payphone butted up to the corner of the store.

"I'll be right back, Bear."

Two directories dangled from the base of the phone. I grabbed the white pages and thumbed through it, tearing out a page when I found what looked to be the correct listing. I needed a map, so I went back into the store and asked the kid if they had any regional map books. He pointed to an aisle full of books, magazines and car accessories. A large regional map book of Charlottesville and its surrounding areas sat next to a rack where the top of every magazine in the row was covered except for its title. I searched the directory in the back of the book, found my street and ripped out the corresponding page.

"Hey," the kid said. "You can't do that."

I walked to the door. "I'm sure the cameras caught it, kid. You can report it."

He yelled again as I pushed through the door. I paid no attention to him. Got in the car and started the engine. Backtracked half a mile and took the bypass around the city. Hopped onto I-64 for a couple miles then exited into a residential area. I turned on the dome light and compared the street names with the map in my hand.

"Where're we going?" Bear asked. He held his right arm tight to his chest. It had been partially numb for the last hour. I began to worry he suffered nerve damage. Not a good thing for his career.

I said nothing and kept my speed steady at forty miles per hour while checking the names on the street signs of every neighborhood we passed. Finally, I found the street I had been looking for and made a right turn into the cookie cutter neighborhood full of two story colonial style houses. It looked like the builder made three models available and decided to follow a model a, then b, then c pattern during construction. I pulled over to the side and stopped next to the curb. The page torn from the white pages sat on my lap. I found the address and compared the house numbers, then turned off the dome light and pulled away from the curb.

"Jack," Bear said, half question, half demand.

"Jessie," I said.

Bear laughed for the first time since being shot. "Kline?" He shifted in his seat to look at me directly. "Jessica Kline?"

I hiked my shoulders a few inches and looked away.

"After what happened to you two?"

I said nothing. After another thirty seconds, I found the house number I'd been looking for, drove half a block past and parked the car next to the curb.

WE STOOD on the front porch for five minutes staring at the red door. Bear leaned back against a post running floor to ceiling, clutching his shoulder, a look of pain spread across his face.

"Knock on the damn door, Jack." His breath formed mist in the air, rising up, enveloping his head before disappearing. "C'mon."

I leaned forward and rapped on the door with my knuckles. A moment later a light flicked on inside. I heard hands tap against the door, the way they would if someone leaned up against it perhaps to listen for a moment.

The porch light turned on and the door cracked open as far as the security chain lock would allow it.

"Who's there?" Jessie asked.

I took a step back and moved over so she could see me through the crack in the door. Our eyes met and locked in a stare that only two former lovers could share.

"Jack?"

"Hey, Jess."

"What're you doing...? Is everything OK?"

"Yeah. No. Can we come in?" I turned sideways and nodded toward Bear. "He's hurt."

"Riley?"

"Heya, Jessie," Bear said.

Jessie closed the door. I heard the sound of the security chain sliding in its lock, and then the door reopened. She stepped back. She wore a white t-shirt and blue sweatpants. She smiled and tucked strands of her dark brown hair behind her ear while extending her other arm in a "come on in" gesture.

I took a step in and stopped in front of her and stared into her dark brown eyes. Opened my mouth to speak, but nothing came out. I had no idea what to say.

She was the first to break off the stare.

"Oh my God," she said. "Riley, what happened to your shoulder?"

"That something you can take care of?" I asked.

She nodded. "Yeah, we get a few gunshot wounds into the ER. I've assisted with enough of them to know what to do." She started toward the other side of the room. "Come to the kitchen."

We followed her through the foyer and living room to the back of the house. Bear entered the kitchen first. The room was painted off white, with a tan tile floor and stainless steel appliances. Dark wood cabinets stretched along three walls and a decorative blue tile back splash stretched between the cabinets and dark granite counter tops.

"Sit," Jessie said, pointing toward the kitchen table. She turned and rifled through a couple drawers under the countertop.

Bear took a seat. I leaned back against the fridge.

"Jack," she said. "Above the fridge, in the cabinet, grab a bottle of whiskey. Put it on the table."

I did as she said, taking a pull from the bottle before setting it down in front of Bear. He let go of his arm, grabbed the bottle and took a pull himself.

Jessie turned in time to witness Bear taking a drink. Her lips stretched into a frown. "That's for your arm."

"You don't have anything else?" Bear asked.

She nodded. "Of course I do. This will numb it a bit, though." She lifted a pair of scissors and cut his sleeve off. She dabbed peroxide onto a hand towel and wiped the blood away from the wound area, then poured peroxide into the hole in Bear's arm.

Bear flinched at first. His face twisted. A moment later he eased up.

Jessie waited until the white fizz from the peroxide settled down, then opened the bottle of whiskey and poured it into the wound.

Bear grimaced and groaned.

"Works fast," Jessie said.

He nodded and sighed.

I reached for the bottle to take another drink. My hand was met by Jessie's as she slapped it away.

"I'm not done," she said.

She grabbed a pair of small forceps off the table. "Riley, grab hold of the table and your chair. Squeeze tight."

He did. His large knuckles turned white.

"Don't break her chair," I said.

Neither of them said anything.

She placed the forceps against the open wound and Bear jumped an inch.

"Steady, Riley, steady." Her voice was low, breathy, soothing.

A shiver of remembrance traveled down my spine. Why I hadn't tried to call or reach out to her during the past five years?

"Now I'm going to extract the bullet," she said. "You ready?" She looked up at Bear.

Bear nodded and forced a loud exhale. He rolled his head to the side and then sat up straight.

She expertly guided the forceps into the wound and grabbed hold of the slug buried in Bear's shoulder, eliciting a groan from the big man as she gripped and pulled the bullet out.

"All done," she said as she dropped the bullet into a glass tumbler. "OK, now I'm going to clean this out and stitch you up."

I stepped out back while she stitched Bear's arm. The cold air hit me with more force than earlier, perhaps an effect of the whiskey, not that I'd had all that much. But it had been such a long couple days that the warming effect of the alcohol gripped me much sooner than it normally would have. I glanced up at the sky, figuring I would get a great view of the stars out here in the country. No such luck though, as gray clouds had overtaken the sky.

The door opened behind me and Jessie poked her head out. "All done in there. Want to come back in?" She smiled. The gesture relaxed me.

I followed her back inside, through the kitchen and into the den. She clicked a black remote and the TV turned on, tuned to one of the twenty-four hour news stations. The sound was low and I couldn't make out what was being said. I didn't need to hear it, though. A familiar face appeared on the screen in the form of a picture.

Delaney.

"Christ," Bear said.

I shook my head, knowing what was coming next.

The picture of Delaney shrunk and moved diagonally down to the side of the screen. My picture was shown next with the words "Armed and Dangerous" flashing underneath and the words "Person of Interest" in a smaller font below.

"Well, at least they got part of it right," I said, turning to Jessie and Bear. "I am a pretty interesting guy."

Bear laughed, Jessie didn't.

"Jack," Jessie said, her voice trailing off at the end. "What's going on?"

I reached out to her. "Jess, you know what I do, right? The whole reason we split up is because..."

The remote dangled from her hand. Her mouth opened, a stutter escaping every few seconds in place of a response.

"Jess, I'm being...we're being set up. That man, Delaney, he was trying to help us. We met at a park. He had information." I reached into my pocket and pulled out the carbineer with the key hanging from it. "This key, Jess, whatever this key unlocks will give me the information I need to clear us."

She shook her head. "Get out." She rose. "Get out. Now. Both of you. Leave."

I got up and placed my hands on her shoulders. She tried to squirm away.

"Look at me, Jess. Look in my eyes."

She stopped shaking her head and lifted her chin, her eyes meeting mine. We engaged in that familiar stare again that said too much had been left unsaid, left undone.

"It's me, Jess. Jack. Look at me and tell me if I'm lying." I looked between her eyes. "I didn't kill Delaney. I'm being set up. The last seventy-two hours have been a cat and mouse game and I'm the mouse." I paused. "Believe me?"

She shook her head. "I don't...I don't know, Jack. You come in here. Bear's all shot up—"

"What happened to 'Riley'?" Bear said.

"— and now this? I just..." She sat back down and curled one foot under her, looked up at me. "I believe you, Jack."

I pulled the wooden coffee table closer and sat on the edge and took her hands in mine. "Thank you." I squeezed her hands. "I'm sorry to have dragged you into this. Don't worry, I'll make sure you're—"

Her phone rang and I shut up and we all turned toward it.

"I better get that." She stood, grabbed the portable phone and disappeared into the kitchen.

THE NEWS COVERAGE continued for another thirty seconds without providing much information. A good thing, I figured. It meant they know much, or someone hadn't fed them much. Yet.

Bear turned to me. "Christ, Jack. We're done for."

"We need to get ahold of Abbot. He can stick his neck out for us."

"The mountains are right there," he said pointing over his shoulder. "We can hide out for a few weeks."

I shrugged and said nothing while waiting for the commercial break to end and the news to return.

Jessie returned a moment later, holding the phone out. "It's for you, Jack."

I grabbed the phone from her hand.

She continued. "Who would know you're here?"

I shook my head and held the phone to my ear. "This is Jack."

There was nothing but silence.

"Hello?" I said.

"Yeah, Jack?"

"Who's this?"

"This is Jack Noble, right?"

"Yeah, who the hell is this?"

There was another pause. I looked around the room, stopping at the two faces staring back at me. Bear sat back in his chair, he looked relieved that he didn't have to hold his shoulder anymore. His clothes were covered in blood. His red cheeks stood out against the rest of his pale face. He held the bottle of whiskey in his hand, brought it up to his lips, took a pull and exhaled loudly.

Jessie forced a smile while tapping with her fingers at the edge of the seat cushion. She crossed, uncrossed, then re-crossed her legs.

"What kind of game are you playing?" I said.

"This is what's going down, Jack." He paused a few seconds, and then continued. "We got you for the murder."

"You know that wasn't me."

"Yeah, well, we got you for it. It's all on you. Pinned on you, Jack." Another pause filled with the sound of the man taking a drink from a bottle. "You can't escape us, Jack. We're everywhere. We know everyone you know. We'll know every move you make a second after you make it. Half the people you know are on our side and the rest can be persuaded by us through one means or another."

I looked between Bear and Jessie, who now stood and paced along the far wall.

"We control everything, Jack."

"Maybe you and I should meet," I said. "Settle this like men. Frankly, I'm tired of the cloak and dagger crap. Know what I mean?"

The man laughed. "You think this is a joke? Listen up. You're going down, Jack. And anyone that helps you is dead. Got that? Even the nurse. Dead as a doornail, Jack."

The line went dead and clicked to dial tone. I looked down at the phone, turned it off. Placed it on the coffee table and walked toward the window. I pinched the bridge of my nose with my thumb and forefinger and slid them down.

"What's going on, Jack?" Bear said.

"We need to go."

The sound of a car racing down the street filled the room. Tires squealed. Car doors opened then slammed shut. The voices of two men drifted in through the open windows.

"Get down."

11

I CUT THE LIGHTS AND MOVED INTO THE NEXT ROOM AND TOOK POSITION against the wall next to the double window. A lace curtain hung over the window panes. I peeled it back and parted the blinds with my fingers. A dark sedan was parked at the end of the driveway. Scanning the yard, I spotted two men, both dressed in dark suits. They didn't appear to be armed, but I wouldn't trust the outward appearance. Armed and dangerous would be the appropriate term. These guys had all the markings of government spooks, Federal agents, maybe even assassins. They hung out at the base of the driveway. One spoke on a radio or cell phone. He stood at an angle and his head blocked the device he spoke into. His other arm waved in circles as he spoke.

I clutched my Beretta M9 tightly. The only thing that stood between me and them was a glass window and I was prepared to break it and open fire if necessary. I went into the woods with two full clips earlier. I'd emptied one and fired three shots from the second. That meant I had twelve rounds at my disposal, which would be more than enough to take care of these guys.

The man with the phone or radio shook his head and stuffed the device in his pocket. He said something to his partner and they both turned to face the house. The window next to me was open a crack, but I couldn't hear what they said. The two men started toward the house, walking slowly. Both pulled their weapons, holding them low with both hands.

I needed a plan and needed it to form fast. There were two men in front which meant that there were probably two out back. There was no way these guys would come here alone. Were they the men from earlier, the shooters in the woods? Had they really managed to follow us to Charlottesville? I guess it was possible, but it didn't add up. The car looked similar, but it was dark now just like it was dark when I rammed the shooters' car while leaving the park.

The only solution I came up with involved me barging out of the house, guns blazing. Not the ideal choice. Getting into a shooting match with trained agents, killers or not, was not high on my priority list. I crouched down and took a look through the open part of the window. I set the barrel of my gun on the window sill. I had a clear shot at them if they took the porch steps. The only barrier was the screen. No glass to break.

The men were close enough that I could make out certain words spoken in hushed tones. They didn't say much, but hearing "Noble" was enough. They knew exactly who I was. They knew exactly where I was. Just like the man on the phone said. Could one of them be the man on the phone? I doubted that. For one, someone that brazen wouldn't be in the field. So it had to be their boss, or their boss's boss.

The faint sound of a cell phone ring-tone filled the air. The men stopped and the agent pulled his phone from his pocket. His voice rose. "What the hell do you mean?" He stepped back during a long pause. "Yeah, OK. OK, we're going." He turned and hurried to the car. His partner walked backward with him. He raised his gun and kept it aimed at the house. He fumbled behind his back for the door handle of the car and then slipped into the driver's seat. The sedan roared to life, then rolled away, stopping at the stop sign at the end of the street only a few houses down. The car turned right and disappeared from view.

I leaned back against the wall and closed my eyes and listened. Silence filled the house. Silence crept through the open window from outside. Had they turned the corner and cut the engine? Were they now on foot returning to the house? Did they leave the neighborhood?

I took a deep breath and returned to the den.

"Can you see the side street from upstairs?"

"What?" Jessie said.

"The side street." I pointed toward the other room. "The main road, whatever. Can you see it from anywhere in here?"

She shook her head and said, "No."

"We have to get out of here. Jess, is your car in the garage?"

"Why?"

"Don't ask me why." My voice rose. I took a deep breath and regained control. "Is it or isn't it?"

She bit her lip and looked to the side.

"Yeah, it's in there."

"OK, grab the keys. We need to go."

"Where?"

"It doesn't matter," I said. "Let's go."

Bear got up and walked toward the kitchen.

"Garage is that way." She pointed to a hall on the other side of the den. "Do I need to bring anything?"

"Yeah." I turned to walk away then paused. "But there's no time. Any minute now they are going to start shooting."

"What?" She grabbed her purse and pulled out her keys, blowing by me and Bear on her way to the garage.

I could be right. Most likely I was wrong. But I had no intentions of waiting around to find out.

I took one last look through the front window, and then, satisfied the spooks weren't out there, went to the garage. I stepped through the open doorway. Bear and Jessie were already inside her white Chevy Tahoe. Bear sat in the passenger seat and Jessie behind the wheel.

"I'm driving," I said, standing in between her and the door, preventing her from shutting it.

"This is my car, Jack," she said. "I'm driving."

"Get in back, Jess."

She screamed and slammed her hands down on the steering wheel. The loud horn blared and echoed throughout the garage.

I shook my head and stared at her. "If they are just around the corner, they likely heard that."

"Sorry," she said and then she threw her hands in the air. "Fine. You drive." She turned in the seat and brought her legs up. Slipped between the two front seats and sat down in the middle row.

"You could have used the door."

"And risk touching you? No thanks." She turned away and stared out the window at a wall covered with rakes and gardening tools.

Bear laughed and shook his head.

"You think that's funny?" I said. "We got God knows who chasing us, ready to kill us, and you laugh at her jokes."

I turned the key in the ignition. The Tahoe's V-8 engine roared into life, flooding my ears as it reverberated through the garage.

Jessie cleared her throat and leaned forward, pointing toward the console on the ceiling of the Tahoe. "The garage door opener is right—"

I ignored her and threw the car into reverse and smashed through the garage door.

"What hell, Jack? My garage!"

I gunned the car down the driveway, slammed on the brakes and turned the wheel, sending us screeching backward into the street. I shifted into drive and raced to the stop sign, coming to a quick halt. I looked left and saw nothing, and then I looked right. I saw the spooks a few blocks away, parked behind Abbot's Audi. At that moment I realized it was the car. They had been tracking us with the car somehow.

I looked over at Bear. He stared out the window at the dark sedan parked behind the Audi. His head bobbed up and down.

"The car," he muttered, reaching the same conclusion as me.

They must not have heard the Tahoe smash through the garage door, because they didn't move or turn to look in our direction. I tapped the gas and turned left and drove down the street with the lights off until I reached the main road.

"WHY DID you destroy my garage door?" Jessie asked.

I looked up into the rearview mirror, taking my eyes off of I-64 for a moment. It was the first thing any of us had said in thirty minutes. Her stare caught me off guard. I started to speak then closed my mouth and said nothing.

"Jack," she said.

"Surprise," Bear said. "He did it for the surprise factor."

"Yeah, well, it worked," she said. "I sure as hell was surprised. Just like he's going to be when I mail the bill to him."

Bear laughed and shook his head. "Not you, Jess. If those feds had been outside your house, the crash would have surprised them. That moment of distraction would have been the difference between us living and dying." He rolled his window down a crack. Wind rushed through the car, the cold air stinging upon impact. "Yeah, we're in this big car, but those guys are trained. One of us would have been hit."

I looked up at the mirror again. A look of knowing washed across Jessie's face. Her eyes teared up. I could tell that the full gravity of the situation had finally hit her and it likely crushed against her chest.

"That was them," she said. "Parked on the side of the street." She looked into the mirror.

I nodded. "Sorry, Jess. We're going to get you someplace safe."

"Safe? How do you know they're not following you now? How—" she pressed her hands into her face and rubbed to the side. "How did they know about me? That was them. The call. Right? How did they know you were at my house?"

"The same reason they knew the car was there." I pulled over on the road's shoulder and stopped the car. Got out and opened her door. "Look at me, Jess. We think...they had a way to track the car. It's the only thing that makes sense."

"No, no it doesn't make sense. They might know the car, but they called for you. Called for you on my phone." By this time she was half out of the car and slamming her fists into my chest.

"There are files on me," I said. "You know what I do and who I am. Well, they do too. They have to know. It's their job to know. When they saw where the car went all they had to do was cross check that against anyone in my file and they found you. That's all. It'll stop there. I promise."

She looked at me with tears in her eyes and shook her head. Her arms lifted over her shoulders and then fell onto me, wrapping around my neck and squeezing tight. A mixture of her tears and hot breath washed over the side of my face. A knot formed in my stomach. I fought back feelings that I hadn't allowed myself to feel in a long time.

I held her tight, running a hand through her hair until she stopped shaking. I let go, turned and got back in the car. The back door slammed and I checked the rearview mirror to make sure she had gotten back in. She had.

"I'm calling Abbot." I pulled out my cell phone, dialed the number and put the Tahoe in gear. The empty road behind me was a green light to jump back on the interstate. I pressed the gas and got the speed up to sixty. Abbot answered as I merged back into the travel lanes.

"Hello?"

"It's Jack."

He said nothing at first. I heard the sound of his fingers or an object banging on a hard surface. I pictured him sitting in his home office, behind his dark cherry wood antique desk. "What happened up there, Jack? You didn't kill Delaney, did you?"

"What do you think?" I didn't kill him, but I couldn't help thinking that, in some way, I was responsible for his death. If I'd have just kept my damn mouth shut in Baghdad, none of this would be happening. I looked up into the rearview mirror and caught Jessie's eye. She smiled, and I looked away.

"I don't think you did, but, well, that's what's being reported on—"

"I know," I interrupted. "I saw the report. It's BS, Abbot. We were ambushed. Delaney was hit in the back of the head. Bear took a slug to the shoulder. I tracked them down through the woods, but they had a car parked at the edge. They took off, and then returned to wait for us outside the parking lot. Managed to get by and fled on the interstate." I paused, thought about whether or not I should tell him about Jessie. I didn't. "The report came on TV. Then someone called for me, not on my number, and next thing I know these two spooks showed up outside at—" I avoided mentioning any names. "Outside the place we stopped to patch Bear up."

There was a pause on the other end. I assumed he was filtering the brief conversation, trying to decide what to believe, who to believe, me or the news. I turned my head and looked at Bear, then shifted my eyes to the rearview mirror to check on Jess. She sat just out of view, resting against the door. I returned my attention to the road. The stretch of interstate heading east toward Richmond, Virginia was empty.

"OK, Jack," Abbot said. "Come to North Carolina. I need you close."

"I'm not returning to Lejeune. If you think that then you can kiss my—"

"Don't come to the base, Jack, for Christ's sake. You think I'm an idiot?" He paused. Was he looking for an answer? Before I could respond, he continued. "Pick a place, but don't tell me where. Some place close enough to Jacksonville that you can be there in a few hours, but far enough away you won't be spotted accidentally." It sounded like he shifted the phone in his hands and changed ears, the phone rubbing against his face with a sound like static as he did so. "Definitely stay far enough away that you won't be made for a Marine."

"You've seen my hair, Abbot. Nobody is going to mistake me for a Marine." I laughed.

He didn't. "This is no time for jokes, son. You two are in serious trouble."

I said nothing. My eyes focused as far out as they could, settling someplace between the road, the mountains and the black darkness of the night sky.

"Some place quiet, Jack. I'm serious." He cleared his throat. "And don't go making a commotion when you get there. Call me in the morning, Jack. First thing."

The line went dead. I dropped the phone in the center console. He wanted us to go someplace quiet. Plenty of places in North Carolina fit that description. He had a point. I'd want to be close enough that I could return to base if necessary. And definitely far enough away that nobody would recognize my face. He didn't say what I knew he was thinking. Stay out of trouble. Whatever you do, stay out of trouble. Don't give the police, or anyone else for that matter, a reason to pick us up. That would be a death sentence wrapped up like a Christmas present under the tree. And the sticker affixed to the wrapping paper would read Jack Noble.

Bear broke the silence a few minutes later. "What'd he say?"

"He said we're in serious trouble."

Jessie leaned forward. "I could have told you that."

Bear started laughing, wincing between outbursts. Jessie joined in, and I did too.

The laughing trailed off. Jessie spoke up. "You think they'll put some kind of broadcast out about my car?"

I looked at Bear who was already shaking his head at me. "They just might."

"

12

FOUR HOURS LATER I TOOK A RANDOM EXIT OFF I-95 JUST OUTSIDE OF ROCKY Mount, North Carolina. That put us about two hours away from Lejeune. Close enough and far enough away all wrapped in one. Bear and Jessie slept. Each had had a rough night of their own. The silence didn't bother me. I welcomed it. It was much better than the uncomfortable silence between me and Jessie when she was awake.

The exit looped in a circle before leading us to a blinking red stoplight. To the left, the road crossed over the interstate toward town. To the right I saw a gas station and not much else. I turned left. The empty road was in stark contrast to the tall neon signs, each shouting, "Stop here for gas, food, coffee and lodging!" Some places had all in one. Nothing looked promising in this section of town, though.

I recalled the sign just before the blinking red light. *Gas .5 miles. Lodging 1.5 miles.* I made a U-turn in the middle of the road. I panicked for a second. Whipping around like that, crossing the median, could be enough for a cop to pull me over and run my ID. How would that look? Big bad Jack Noble taken down by a country cop for making an illegal U-turn. I shook my head and grinned. The rearview mirror revealed no such encounter would take place tonight, at least not yet.

We rolled across the interstate overpass, past the open-all-night 24-hour gas station. The motel appeared suddenly after a curve in the road. The neon sign placed near the parking lot entrance blinked on and off. When switched on, it read "vacancy," which was enough to convince me to pull into the parking lot.

I parked the Tahoe by the front office then opened the door and hopped out of the vehicle and made my way around the front. I heard another car door open and close. Jessie made her way to the lobby entrance and waited for me.

"You don't need to come in," I said.

She shrugged. "Tired of sitting."

"It's best you're not seen with me."

"Whatever, I'm going in."

I opened the door and gestured her through first. A middle-aged man with a shaved, pointed head sat behind the desk. He propped his chin upon his open palm, fingers wrapping back along his jawline to his ear. He opened his eyes and blinked repeatedly at the chiming of the string of bells hanging from the door, shaking and clattering together as we walked into the small dimly lit lobby. It smelled like mildew and pine tree car air fresheners. The odor lingered in the back of my throat.

The desk clerk stood up and tugged at the shirt hugging his barreled chest, straightening it out. "How can I help y'all?"

"Need a room for a couple nights," I said.

"Two rooms," Jessie said.

"No," I leaned against the counter and turned my head to her, leaning in so we were eye to eye. "One room." I emphasized each word equally.

"Excuse me," she said, poking a finger in my chest. "If you think I'm about to spend the night in the same room as you and your partner—"

I placed my hand on her shoulder. "Jess, think about this for a minute." Out of the corner of my eye I could see that the desk clerk had placed an arm on the counter and was leaning over it, a smile on his face. "We'll talk outside." I stood and turned toward the clerk. "One room. Two beds. Three nights."

The clerk stood, sniffed and wiped his nose with his sleeve. "That'll be two hundred fifty."

I pulled a wad of cash from my wallet and dropped it on the counter.

"We don't take cash," he said.

I pulled out another fifty, dropped it next to the pile of cash.

"Ok, room 114, 'round back." He slid two keys across the counter.

We turned and left the lobby. The moment the door closed behind us, Jessie ripped into me.

"What the hell was that, Jack?" She jockeyed for position in front of me, walking backwards and poking me in the chest. "I don't know what you are thinking, but if you think, for one moment, that you and I are going to—"

"I don't think any of that," I said. "Damn, what the hell do you think is going on here? You are riding with two fugitives. We got CIA, MPs, and probably the damn NSA on us. You want to be in a room by yourself when those guys show up? Do you?" I stepped back and turned sideways, extending my arm toward the lobby door. "Well then march right in there and get your own damn room."

She opened her mouth to speak, but said nothing. She threw her arms in the air, turned and got back in the Tahoe.

I smiled and then climbed back inside and turned the key in the ignition.

"Just like old times," Bear said.

"Shut up," Jess and I said at the same time.

I shifted into drive and pulled around the back of the building, parking in a spot a few rooms down from ours. I wanted to leave as much visibility through the front windows as I could. I didn't like the fact that we were at the back of the building. The only thing it had going for it was that we weren't in the front, and were shielded from the road. But the positive fed right into the negative. We could easily be ambushed.

I put the key into the door and turned the knob. Felt along the wall to the left until I found a light switch. A dim, yellowish overhead light flickered on and off for a few seconds before staying on and flooding the room. The room was barely larger than the lobby and had the same moldy, pine-tree infused smell.

Bear pushed in from behind me. "Five star all the way, Jack."

I shrugged.

"Seriously, man. Weren't there better options in town?"

"Yeah." There were. But there were also more people in town. More cops in town. More chances of being spotted in town. "We're national celebrities right now, Bear. Further we are from town the better."

"I suppose," he said, moving to claim a bed for himself.

"You two bunking together?" Jessie asked.

I spun on my heel, ready to rip into her for the remark. She stood inches from me, looking up and smiling. The yellow light above us reflected off her dark brown eyes. Her olive complexion absorbed the light and radiated it outward.

"What?" she said. "No witty comebacks?"

I forced a smile. I felt a burning inside that had disappeared a long time ago. I wanted to be with her again. Lean in and kiss her. Make love to her. Talk all night afterward.

"Ja-ack," she said, singing my name. "Snap out of it." Her hand slapped across my face lightly.

I smiled without having to force it and took a step back. "I'm going toward town. Saw a store that was open on the way in. Need to grab a few things." I moved to the door, opened it and stopped. "Keys to the Tahoe are on the nightstand if you need them."

"You're not taking it?" Bear asked.

"No," I said. "I need to take a walk."

THE WIND PICKED up during my walk and the cold night air bit at my face. It stung. It felt good. The country air and peaceful surroundings gave way to the sound of vehicles traveling on I-95. Families on vacation for spring break, business people driving overnight for their morning meetings, and truckers making the long haul from Florida to New York then back again. I filtered the sound of the traffic in my mind and allowed my brain to distort it. It reverberated through the air like waves at the beach. That calm feeling washed over me again. I laughed at myself for being able to relax with everything that had occurred in the last few days and the probable consequences hanging over me.

I followed the winding road through a stretch of woods. A tall bright signpost appeared front and center as I stepped past the wooded stretch.

Two cars were parked next to gas pumps. A middle-aged man walked a golden retriever in the patch of grass between the gas station's parking lot and a closed diner.

I crossed the street and stopped in front of the store entrance to think for a minute, using the time to acclimate myself to the store's surroundings.

The man with the golden retriever returned to his mini-van and opened the back door. The dog jumped in the back seat, cuddling up to a little girl. The man nodded at me and jogged to the driver's side of the car. A minute later the car turned left out of the parking lot and turned right onto the interstate on-ramp, disappearing from sight.

I opened the door to the store, a single chime greeting me as I walked through the open doorway.

"Hello," a cheerful young woman said from behind her register. She was dressed in black pants, a white button up shirt, and wore a red and white checkered vest. A red tag had the name Michelle printed on it in white lettering with a black outline. She wore her dark hair in a ponytail and wore too much make-up, perhaps to cover the ever-present dark circles under her eyes and the premature lines on her face from a lifetime of working odd shifts at places like this. Or maybe places even worse.

I nodded and looked away.

"Looking for anything specific?"

"No. I'll just be a few minutes."

She put her hands on the counter, slumped over and frowned, all the while nodding her head. "Okies. I'll be here when you're done."

She must live for moments when someone would come into the store in the middle of the night and carry on a conversation with her.

I grabbed a hand basket and wove my way up and down the aisles, grabbing various items as I went. I had no idea what I wanted. Just needed to pass the time and clear my head. Jessie had thrown me for a loop at the motel. Now wasn't the time for me to think about relationships and life after the military. And not just because of the current predicament I found myself in. It went beyond that. The life I led, and the life I foresaw myself leading for some time to come, left no room for love and relationships. Those things were liabilities in my world, not assets.

The basket grew heavy. I looked down and saw I had filled it to the top.

That was my cue that I'd grabbed enough off the stocked shelves. I walked to the counter and placed the basket on it.

"Anything else?"

I looked around at the display to the side and shook my head. "No, this'll be all."

She babbled on, but her words didn't register in my head. I stared out the window at a group of four men cutting through the parking lot to the store. A couple of them yelled at an elderly man filling his car with gas. The old man cut it short, hung the nozzle up at the pump and got in his car, driving off in a hurry. The men laughed and slapped hands and pointed at the store.

"—and so I'm only doing this until I have enough saved to go back to college and then I'll—"

"You know those men?" I gestured with my head toward the window.

Michelle bit her lip and nodded.

"Troublemakers?"

"One of them's my ex," she said. "And he's not a nice guy. Ex-con."

"What'd he do?"

She looked up from her scanner and the item in her hand. Her eyes watered over. "Tried to kill me." She wiped her eyes with her sleeve. "You should go. Just take the stuff and go. Those guys are bad news, especially if they've been drinking."

"Keep ringing this stuff up. Don't say anything to them. Don't acknowledge them. Got it?"

She said nothing.

The electronic chime rang when one of the men pulled the front door open. They stepped through one at a time and cut to the left, behind me, laughing as they walked down the aisle. I got a good glimpse at them as they came through. All dressed the same, old jeans, black Doc Martin combat boots, and heavy flannel shirts worn as jackets. Two had long hair, one had a shaved head, and the fourth kept his cut close on the side and spiked four inches on top. Only the bald man came close to matching me in size, but that didn't mean I'd underestimate any of them. You never knew what a man was capable of until the moment of impact.

"This your new boyfriend, Michelle?"

She looked at me and said nothing then glanced down at the empty basket on the counter.

I looked up at the small TV fed by the security camera. The group of men approached from behind.

I turned around, held my arms out to the side, resting my elbows on the counter. I made eye contact with the bald man leading the group.

He stopped six feet away from me. Far enough away that he could escape if I made a move. His guys fanned out, two toward the door, one on the other side. The bald man leaned to the side, looking around me. "Michelle, you hear me?"

Her breathing picked up. She said nothing.

"Bitch," he said. "You better answer me." He looked at me and then at her. He started to redden, first his neck and cheeks, then the rest of his pale face.

"I think," I straightened up, "you should apologize and then leave."

"Screw you, Jarhead."

Jarhead? How could he tell? I looked nothing like a Marine. "I'm not looking for any trouble tonight—"

"Yeah, well you just found some." He took a step forward.

Keep it coming, baldy.

"—I think you should turn around and go home. Sleep it off. Hell, go down to the highway and play *Frogger* with the semis for all I care. Probably do the world a favor."

His eyes narrowed as he processed what I said. He looked to the side, toward the door, and laughed. Two seconds later he was in my face.

I didn't flinch.

He did his best scary guy impersonation, shoulders back, face inches from mine. He exhaled heavily through his mouth. I could have gotten drunk on his hot alcohol-stained breath if he stayed there long enough.

"What you got to say now?" he said.

My hand moved to one of the displays on the counter. I fingered a few items until I felt that I had the item I wanted. I smiled then brought my hand forward. "I think you could use a breath mint."

One of the guys behind him laughed. The bald man turned. "Shut the hell up." He took a few steps back, never taking his eyes off of me. He started to shift from his left to his right foot and back. Was he contemplating his next move? Preparing to hit me? Turn and run? He probably didn't expect me to stand my ground like I had, with no sign of fear on my face. Sure the feeling was there, but I'd learned to control fear a long time ago.

"Mike, let's go," the one with spiky hair said. "Cameras in here, man. You ain't s'posed to be near Michelle, anyway."

Mike took a few more steps back and went to the door. Stopped and turned to face me again. "This ain't over. Got it?"

"Yeah it is, Mike," I said. "Now get the hell out of here before I mop the floor with your face."

The men left the store. Mike stopped in the open doorway, pointed at me then pounded his chest twice with his fist. The door slammed shut behind him. He jogged across the parking lot, holding his pants up with one hand, and caught up with his friends. They walked past the glow of the gas station lights and the night swallowed them whole.

"I-I'm sorry about that," Michelle said.

I waved her off. "Don't be. I'm not worried about those guys." I leaned over the counter. "I am worried about you though. You should probably lock up and leave."

She shook her head. "They won't be back. Besides, I'd get fired if I did that."

"They could be. And fired is better than dead."

"They're just drunk. He'll apologize in the morning. He's," she paused and turned toward the front of the store. "He's not supposed to get within one hundred yards of me. One call and he'll go to jail. He knows that. He'll apologize in the morning." A tear rolled down her cheek.

I shook my head. Was there any point in trying? She'd made up her mind about the guy. I knew then that she eventually planned to go back to him. And one day, she'd likely pay with her life.

"Keep your eye out. Call 9-1-1 the moment you see them."

She nodded then looked away.

I dropped a hundred dollar bill on the counter, picked up the bag she'd filled with my items, and started toward the door.

"Hey," she said.

I turned back to her.

"Don't you want your change?"

"Keep it."

I pushed through the door. The cold air hit me like a baseball bat. Beads of sweat felt like tiny icicles as they dried on my skin. I crossed the parking lot diagonally and continued across the street. Five minutes later the roar of a diesel engine filled the air. It wasn't until the engine idled lower that I became concerned. The truck slowed to a near stop next to me.

"Yep, that's him," a voice said from inside the cab.

The truck lurched forward. Red taillights illuminated the immediate area as the truck jerked sideways and screeched to a stop in front of me. Four doors opened. Four men stepped out. The two longhaired rednecks were the first to approach. One held a shotgun. Mike stepped around the one on the driver's side of the truck.

"Hello again," Mike said. "Remember us?"

13

Mike stood at the back of the truck, seven or eight feet away from me. His eyes were wide, his body slightly hunched over. He clenched and unclenched his fists a dozen times. A wide smile spread over his face. The man with the gun was to his left, on the shoulder of the road. The other two men moved toward the field. I expected one to stop when even with me and the other to continue behind me. Of course, these guys were amateurs, which meant anything was possible.

I stood my ground. I wouldn't make the first move unless forced to. Something told me that wouldn't be an issue, though.

The gunman shifted side to side. He was jumpy and sweat beaded on his forehead even though a nice breeze blew cool air into his face. Was this his first time pointing a gun at someone? Or the first time he did so with the intention of pulling the trigger? Either way, it concerned me. I had to take him out first.

The heft of my Beretta pressing against my side felt reassuring. I preferred to not use it, though. Not for those guys. I only had twelve bullets left and the way this day was going, I was sure I'd need them before the sun came up.

"Well?" Mike said.

I said nothing, keeping my focus on him and the gunman.

"Aw c'mon, Jarhead," Mike said. "Ain't you got nothing funny to say?"

"No," I said. "You just said it for me."

"Huh?"

His smile faded and he squinted at me. It looked like he struggled to make sense of what I said.

The gunman didn't. A wry smile formed on his face and his eyes shifted between me and Mike.

"By the time you figure it out, you'll be unconscious. So it might benefit you to concentrate on the task at hand."

The gunman threw his head back and laughed.

At least one of them had a sense of humor, or maybe he had smoked enough pot that I could say anything and he would laugh. I thought about testing this theory out by throwing some nonsense at him, but it made more sense to throw a shoulder into his gut. I had two seconds, maybe three, before his senses would return and he'd take aim. Another second at the most between him aiming and pulling the trigger. Unless he really was stoned, in which case, double those times.

The width of the truck separated Mike and the gunman. Mike stood slightly behind the bumper and the gunman near the corner.

I lunged at the gunman. One hand aimed at this throat, the other at the barrel of the gun. I needed to disable and disarm him at the same time. I took two steps before he opened his eyes. My left fist crashed into the soft spot of his throat about the same time recognition flashed in his eyes. I grabbed the barrel of the gun and twisted it so that his wrist bent unnaturally backward.

The gunman gasped and gargled for air. He steadied himself by placing his free arm on the lip of the truck bed.

I struck again with my left arm, driving my elbow into his nose. I delivered a swift kick to his kneecap. He went down and let go of the shotgun. I spun and stepped back toward the road, aiming the gun at the group of men approaching me.

Mike stood in the middle flanked by the other two men. The gunman rolled on the ground next to me, clutching his throat and sucking in whatever bits of air he could squeeze into his shriveling lungs.

"Don't move," I said.

The moon glinted off the blade of the serrated edge hunting knife in Mike's hand.

"Drop the knife or lose your hand," I said.

"Screw you," he said.

I studied his face. His upper lip curled and his cheek quivered. He looked crazy enough to charge me with the knife extended. I had a decision to make. Take the truck and haul ass, or shoot and add to my already inflated murder count. I aimed the shotgun and fired into the air over their heads.

The knife fell to the ground.

I emptied the gun and moved toward the men. Mike stepped up. I drove the butt of the gun into his stomach and followed it up with a smack across his head. He fell to the ground. The other two men came at me together. I kicked the spiky-haired man in the gut. He doubled over. I smashed the butt of the gun into the back of his head. The fourth man pulled a knife. I tossed the gun into the bed of the truck. The odds were already against the longhaired man.

"I'm going to cut you, man," he said. "Then I'm going to slice your gut open."

His words sounded tough. But his twitching and shaking revealed how scared he was.

I didn't waste any time. I took a step toward him. Blocked his swipe at me and took control of his wrist. I spun inward and drove my elbow into the bridge of his nose.

He grunted and went limp. The knife dropped to the ground. I darted toward it and scooped it up.

I heard a voice speak up from behind me. "You and me."

I spun around and saw Mike standing six feet away, knife in his hand. Blood covered his forehead and split into three lines at his eyebrows. The streams of blood poured down his face. He wiped his sleeve across his eyes. Blood smeared across his cheeks.

"You don't want to do this," I said.

"Scared?"

"For you."

He laughed then spit. "You don't know me, man."

"Sure I do," I said. "I know all about you. I've run into bitches like you every place I've ever been."

He said nothing. He stuck his arm out and lunged toward me.

I stepped to the side and watched him slip by and fall to the ground.

Mike got to his knees and turned as he stood. He approached again, this time slowly and cautiously.

He brought his hands up and flipped the knife around in his hand to a tactical fighting position. The kind of position they teach in advanced combat training. Had he been a Marine or in the Army? Is that how he pegged me so easily? He stepped in and took a swipe at me.

I countered and played defense while he attacked. He'd already taken a couple heavy blows from me. He might have a few broken ribs and a concussion. All I had to do was wear him down and then knock him out.

I kept an eye on his friends in between his attacks. Only one stirred, but he wasn't a threat, yet.

"Attack me," Mike said. "C'mon."

I said nothing. His attack was weak and easy to counter. He might have had training but it had either been a long time ago, or it had not been very advanced.

He broke pattern and swung wildly, opening himself up to a counterattack. I took advantage of the opening and sliced then stabbed, first into his side and then his shoulder. I took care to avoid any major organs and arteries. Despite this guy's overwhelming sense of asshole, I didn't want his death hanging over me.

The strike to his shoulder did enough damage to cause him to drop the knife.

I kicked him from behind. He crashed head first into the truck's liftgate. Fell to the ground. He got to his hands and knees and then, using the truck to help him, stood. He was shaky at first and slowly steadied.

Cars had passed during the fight. A few slowed down, but none stopped to help or intervene. One of them must have notified the police, because I heard sirens approaching.

Mike turned his head at the sound. He looked back at me and smiled.

"What the hell are you smiling at?" I said.

"You're going down, Jarhead. I'm untouchable here."

I hiked my shoulders up an inch and let out a quick laugh before taking a step forward and whipping my right fist across his face. The thud of my fist connecting with his head coincided with the snapping sound of his jaw breaking. He fell back onto the truck. His head rolled forward. His eyes rolled backward. He collapsed on the ground in front of me.

I looked over my shoulder and saw blue lights reflecting off the sky. My cue to leave. I cut through the field and sprinted toward the trees. I ran blind until I was hidden in the cover of the woods, and even then my pace didn't slow down.

"Jack," Jessie said as I burst through the door. "What the hell happened to you?"

I looked in the mirror mounted over the dresser and noticed four cuts on my face and several on my arms. My adrenaline had been pumping so high, I didn't realize I had received the injuries while running through the woods.

"Jack?"

I spoke between breaths. "Took a jog through the woods."

Bear lifted his head. "Why?"

I fell back onto the bed and stared at the yellow tinted popcorn ceiling.

Nobody spoke.

After a few minutes I went to the door and looked through the window next to it. "Bear, can you go around front and see if any cop cars are out there?"

"Cop cars?" he said. "What the hell did you do?"

I crossed the room and stopped outside the bathroom door. "I got jumped."

"Then why were you running?"

"The cops were coming."

"Again, why did you run?" Bear asked.

"Something the guy said," I said. "He said he was untouchable."

Bear shook his head. He got up and moved into my field of vision. "What happened?"

"That's not all," I said. "He made me for a Marine."

Bear shrugged. He hunched over and we were eye to eye. He nodded slowly and changed facial expressions repeatedly, like he was thinking about saying something but was stuck searching for the right words.

"Just go check out front," I said. "Stay out of view, though. There were four of them and only two are hurt enough to go to the hospital."

He moved to the door. Turned back and nodded, then stepped outside. The door closed with a thud.

I looked at Jessie. She smiled, but her furrowed brow gave her away.

"Jess," I said. "I'm sorry I got you involved in this. I wasn't thinking when we stopped—"

She waved me off. "I'm glad you showed up."

"Are you kidding? Your life might be ruined. Is ruined."

She crossed the room and stood in front of me. Placed her hands on my shoulders and leaned in. I felt her hot breath on my neck. "My life's been ruined since I walked out of yours."

I leaned back. Our eyes met and locked in that familiar stare. She brushed her lips against mine and held them close. We kissed. My stomach tensed and eased. I was transported back in time for a moment.

She pulled back and dragged her hand down the side of my face.

I winced as her nails crossed a cut on my face.

"I'm sorry," she said, leaning in to kiss the wound.

"It doesn't hurt."

She smiled, stood and grabbed my hands, pulling me to my feet. "C'mon. Let's get you cleaned up."

I stood and our bodies pressed together momentarily. She smiled and turned.

I followed her into the bathroom and closed the door behind me. She turned the faucet on. I spun her around and grabbed her by the waist. Lifted her onto the sink and leaned in to kiss her. She kissed me back. Our hands rediscovered each other. I pulled away.

"What's wrong?" she asked.

"Bear," I said.

"Why are you thinking about Bear? Don't tell me I was right about you two?" A smile formed on her lips as she winked.

I grabbed her hands and pulled them together, resting them on my chest. "He's going to be back any minute."

"Send him out again."

"Too risky. This place is not safe."

She sighed and leaned forward, placing her head on my shoulder, lips against my neck. "Should have rented two rooms."

I stepped back and lifted her chin with my finger. We stared into each other's eyes for a few moments.

"I have to fix this," I said.

"Fix what?"

"This situation. I have to clear our names. Something stinks and I need to get to the bottom of it. But I promise, I'll fix it."

She tucked her bottom lip inside her mouth and let it slowly roll back out from under her front teeth.

"Is that all that needs fixing?"

I leaned in and kissed her again. "I want to fix us, too."

She smiled.

"I'm done after this. Done with the Marines, the agency, the life." I turned around and walked to the door. Stopped and looked back at her. "I want to come home to you."

———

"WHERE HAVE YOU BEEN?" I said to Bear when he opened the door and stepped back into the room.

"Relax," he said. "Just checking things out."

"How is it?"

"Seems calm," he said. "But the cops are everywhere, up and down the street, Jack. We should think about getting out of here."

I went to the door. "I'm calling Abbot."

The wind had picked up since I ran back to the motel. The tall grasses behind the motel rustled in the breeze, filling the air with a hissing sound. I followed the wall to a corner and peeked around. Empty. Moved into the corridor between the buildings so I could get a look at the parking lot, which was empty as well. I pulled out my cell phone and found Abbot's number. He answered midway through the third ring.

"Hello?" Abbot said. His raspy voice indicated I'd woken him.

"It's Jack," I said. "I'm sorry to wake you. We're in trouble."

"Where are you?"

"We're—" I debated whether or not I should tell him. I didn't. "Don't worry about that," I said. "We've got to move. But I need to run something by you first."

He grunted into the phone. "Where are my damn glasses," he said under his breath. "Jack, you remember the lake house?"

"Outside Wilson?"

"Yeah."

"I think I can find it."

Wilson, NC wasn't too far from where we were, just a short drive down I-95, not even thirty miles away.

"That's where I'm at now. Come out here. I've got something else for you."

"OK," I said. "We'll be there within an hour."

Abbot said goodbye and hung up.

I stuffed the phone back into my pocket. I stopped outside the motel room and leaned against the vinyl siding between the door and window. I thought about Jessie and what she might be thinking. Having her around felt like home, and I felt like myself again. The Jack Noble I was before I left for the Marines, before I agreed to become part of this damn joint program with the CIA, before I became a killer.

The wind whipped the clouds across the sky and revealed a blue canopy with pinholes of starlight illuminating through the fabric of the universe. I grew tired of the cold and entered the room.

"Well?" Bear asked.

"He's close by," I said. "We can go. It's a safe place."

Bear nodded and Jessie stood next to the door, her hand on the knob.

We piled into the Tahoe. I started the ignition and drove along the narrow road that ran the length of the motel in between the building and the empty field. I rounded the corner and drove across the main parking lot. Pulled out onto the road and headed toward I-95.

"You think it's safe to get on the interstate?" Bear asked.

I shrugged. It might not be, but that was the quickest way that I knew to get where we needed to go. "We'll be all right."

A row of blue lights came streaming toward us in the opposite lane. I turned my attention to the rearview mirror after they passed by.

"Think they're going to the motel?" Bear asked.

"Yeah," I said.

"How?"

"No clue."

My phone rang and I pulled it out of my pocket and glanced at the display.

"General Keller."

I started to answer, but stopped and looked at Bear. Keller would have to wait.

"The phone."

We said it at the same time.

"For Christ's sake," I said.

I stopped the car, stepped out and threw the phone as far as I could. It landed on the other side of the overpass with a thud, skidding along the asphalt and coming to rest out of sight.

14

Tall trees wrapped around Abbot's lake house on all four sides. A winding gravel driveway and a simple path to the lake provided the only break in the ring. The trees kept the wind out. Despite the cool air, sweat formed on my brow as I stood on the porch and knocked on the door.

The porch light flicked on and the door opened. Abbot nodded and stepped back, waving us inside.

I scanned the room. Not much different from the last time I was here. Two full-sized dark leather couches were placed in the middle of the room and faced each other. A table made from the wide trunk of a tree was placed in between the couches. An old recliner nestled up to the corner of the room. A big flat panel TV hung from the wall. That was new.

Abbot caught me staring at the TV. "That was a gift. Once everyone found out, they all wanted to come up here on Sundays to watch the game." He smiled and shook his head. "Can I get you all anything? Food? Drink?"

"I'll have a beer," Bear said. "No denying that I need one."

Abbot disappeared through an opening to the kitchen.

Bear and Jessie sat on opposite couches. I stood by the front door.

Abbot returned a few minutes later carrying a six pack of beer and a pizza box. Smoke escaped where cardboard edges met. The smell of cheese and tomatoes and dough lingered in the air. He set the beer and the pizza box on the tree trunk table. Then he opened the box and gestured toward it.

"It got here a few minutes before you three. Eat what you want." He sat down on the same couch as Jessie, leaning back into the corner and placing his feet on the table. "I've got two spare rooms. Divvy them up how you see fit." His eyes shifted from me to Jessie, then back to me. He smiled.

Jessie looked over at me and smiled as well.

"Don't know how much I can sleep," I said. "Once all this is over I'm probably going to spend a week in bed."

Bear laughed. Through a mouthful of pizza he said, "You speak the truth, Jack."

Abbot smiled through tightly drawn lips. He crossed and uncrossed his arms. His facial expressions changed often, and he drew his brows tight over his eyes while his lips pressed together. I caught him looking at me several times, and instead of keeping eye contact, he'd look away.

"We need to talk," I said.

Abbot nodded and set his feet on the floor. He put a hand down on the arm of the couch and pushed himself up.

"Follow me to my study."

Bear dropped half a piece of pizza in the box and leaned forward to get up.

"Stay out here," I said as I held my hand out toward him. "Stay with Jess."

Bear shrugged, grabbed his pizza and leaned back on the couch.

I followed Abbot out of the room and down a hallway. We said nothing. When we came to a set of six stairs, he turned and climbed them. I did the same. He reached the top and flicked on a light.

"Room's new," I said.

"Yeah," he said. "Built it last year. My study." He shuffled some papers on his antique cherry wood desk. "Clarissa calls it my grandpa room," he added.

"Is that right," I said. "She has a kid now?"

He shook his head and looked down at his desk over his arms folded across his chest. He then leaned back in his leather chair.

"No, and I prefer she keep it that way. That girl has no business raising a child at this point in her life. Not after being raised by me."

"How old is she now?"

"Nineteen."

I pulled the key attached to the carbineer clip from my pocket and tossed it on his desk.

"That's what I got from your contact."

He pulled open a desk drawer and reached in.

I fought the urge to reach for my gun.

He lifted his eyes in my direction while keeping his face pointing down.

"Just getting my glasses, Jack."

I nodded and sat back in my chair.

He pulled a thin pair of gold rimmed glasses from the desk drawer and put them on. They slid down his nose and he readjusted them with his thumb. The key sat on a white notepad. He picked it up and studied it.

"What's it for?" he asked.

"Don't know. Bullet ripped through his head before he could tell me." I leaned forward, interlaced my fingers and rested my elbows on my knees. "I was hoping you would know."

Abbot shook his head and tossed the key back toward me. "What do you think it unlocks?"

"Whatever is holding the documents? Look, Abbot, I don't know what these documents contain, but it must be some heavy stuff for someone to take out Delaney like that. Not to mention follow me all the way down here."

Abbot lifted an eyebrow. "They found you down here?"

I shook my head, stopped and shrugged my shoulders. "I can't be sure. I went out. Ran into some rednecks. One of them struck me as odd. The way he placed me as a Marine, and said he was untouchable."

Abbot's eyes narrowed. He pulled out his cell phone and placed it on the desk.

"That's another thing," I said. "I am pretty sure they were tracking me through my phone."

He sat up. "You didn't bring it here, did you?"

"No. I jettisoned it before we got back on the interstate."

L.T. RYAN

Abbot picked up the phone and spun it in his palm. "I need you to wait outside the room for a few minutes, Jack. I need to make a call."

I stood up. "Before I go…"

"Yeah?"

"You talk to Keller yet? He finally called me back, but that was when I realized they were tracking through the phone."

"No, I haven't heard from him yet. We can call him after I make this call."

I WAITED IN THE HALLWAY, halfway between Abbot's study and the living room. Bear and Jessie talked quietly in between bites of pizza and swigs of beer. The heat cut off and the house fell still. I leaned back against the wall and closed my eyes. I felt calm and relaxed. For the first time in days I felt like I could lie down on the floor and sleep for six hours straight.

I paced the hall. Smiled at Bear from the end and turned back and walked the other direction. A series of pictures in a single frame hung neatly in the middle of the hall. Most were of Abbot's daughter, Clarissa. The pictures were a chronology of her growing up. It had been three years since I last saw her. She'd made it past the gangly young teenager stage and had looked like a woman. Half the pictures were from then or before. The last picture looked to be the most recent, and she appeared to be quite grown up now. Her bright red hair had darkened and the freckles on her cheeks and nose faded.

Bear called from the other room. I walked down the hall toward the sound of his voice. Thirty seconds after I stepped into the living room I heard a crash and the sound of glass breaking. I froze in place for what seemed like minutes. I turned to run down the hall. A gunshot rang out and echoed down through the house.

"Get her away from the windows," I shouted to Bear.

I raced down the hallway, drew my gun and kicked open the door to the study. Immediately I rolled to my right and backed up to the wall next to the open doorway. I led with my Beretta and peeked around the corner, up the stairs.

124

"Abbot," I called.

He said nothing. It was quiet and a cool breeze flowed through the open doorway.

I took each step slowly, one at a time. Once eye level to the floor, I scanned the room. The only person I saw was Abbot. He was on the floor in front of his desk. I looked to the wall and saw the broken window. A jagged hole in the middle told me that the gunman had most likely stood outside the window, jammed his gun through and fired. How long had he been waiting out there for the perfect shot? Was he there when I was in the room, my back to the window? I ran my hand over the back of my head.

Abbot lay on the floor. His eyes fluttered. His breaths were short and rapid. Blood pooled below him, leaking from a hole in his chest.

"Jessie," I called down the stairway and through the open doorway.

I walked over to the window. A risky move, given that it was pitch black outside and light inside. Whoever did this didn't stay around, though. They would have stormed the house if they were after me. I had the feeling that this was a hit on Abbot.

And it was my fault.

Bear and Jessie entered the room.

"Cut the lights downstairs and turn on whatever outside lights you can find, Bear."

Jessie hunched over Abbot, applying pressure to the wound. "Call 9-1-1."

I walked back to Abbot, dropped to my knees next to his head.

He sucked in air, his head bobbing an inch, and tried to speak. His mouth worked hard to form the words.

"Jack."

I leaned in close to his head.

He took two short gasps.

"F-F-Find C-Clarissa." He paused for more air. "Watch over her for..." The words trailed off.

I took his hand in mine and cradled his head with my other hand. "I will, Colonel."

"Th-the desk."

His body went slack.

"Help me perform CPR," Jessie said.

I stood, looked around the room and then at the desk.

"Jack," she said.

"There's no point, Jess. Look at him."

She ignored me and went to work trying to revive Abbot. The words "lost cause" meant nothing to her.

I stepped over her and moved to the back of the room and stopped and stood behind Abbot's desk. What did he want me to find there? I went through each drawer one at a time not knowing what to look for. The drawers were organized, each having its own purpose. One had pens, markers, paper clips and other office supplies. Two were empty. The third contained a few file folders housing documents pertaining to the property. There was no actual file cabinet. The house served as Abbot's weekend home and he likely did very little in terms of work while here.

My eyes scanned the desktop. Back and forth I looked for anything that wasn't there when I sat across the desk from Abbot. Nothing seemed out of the ordinary. There was his computer monitor, an award of some sort, his desk calendar, and a picture of Abbot and Clarissa when she was a little girl. He held two fishing poles and she held up a nice-sized largemouth bass.

Jessie rose from the other side of the desk. Her blood-covered hands hung by her side. Tear-stained cheeks were red with frustration. She shook her head and looked down at the floor. She blew upwards to get a strand of hair out of her face.

"I'm sorry, Jack."

"I know. Nothing you could do, Jess. This is my fault."

"No, Jack. Don't say that."

"I called him. We showed up. Half an hour later he's dead. Hard to ignore the damn pattern."

She said nothing. Her eyes scanned the desktop.

"I need to get you someplace safe. You're in danger with me."

"What are you looking for?" she asked, ignoring everything I had just said.

"He said, 'the desk.'" I gestured across the six-foot long, three foot wide desktop. "So I'm looking on the desk."

"Maybe inside the desk?"

I shook my head. "I checked. Nothing that made sense in there."

She started to speak, and stopped after letting out an *ah* sound.

"What is it?"

She hesitated and bit the left side of her bottom lip. She lifted her head and initiated eye contact. "202."

"What?"

She reached out and pointed at the calendar.

"202."

I followed her hand. There it was, 202, followed by a dash, three more numbers and another dash followed by three more numbers.

"202 is D.C.," she said. "It's a phone number. Missing a digit, but still a phone number."

"And a name," I said. "Look." I put my finger down on the calendar next to the name and number. "Conners."

"Who is that?" she asked.

"I don't know," I said. "It's either who Abbot was talking to or who he was being referred to."

Jessie nodded.

"I need to find him." I tore off the section of the calendar with the name and number and stuck it in my pocket, then gestured to Jessie to follow me.

Bear met us in the living room. "We should go, Jack."

I nodded. I had a feeling the police would show up soon. Whoever did this would try to frame me for it. My prints were all over the house by this point, and we had no time to clean up.

"Go start the car," I said. "I'm going to take a quick look around."

Bear ran to the door. His heavy steps reverberated through the floor. He left the house.

"Should I go outside?" Jessie asked.

"Stay with me." I led her into the kitchen. "Look for bottled water and food we can take with us."

She scavenged the kitchen while I checked the table, drawers and cupboards. A phone hung on the wall. A piece of paper was held in place behind a piece of plastic above the number pad. The paper contained a few names and numbers. My name was there, so was Keller's. That wasn't what I was looking for though. At the top of the list was the name Clarissa. Next to her name was a 212 phone number. New York City. I popped the plastic off the phone, grabbed the piece of paper and stuffed it in my pocket. I checked over my shoulder. Jess didn't seem to notice.

"We can go," I said.

I left the kitchen with Jessie following behind.

Bear stood in the open doorway blocking our exit to the outside.

"Everything all right?" I asked.

"Yeah," he said.

"Let's go then."

"It's too all right, Jack."

"What do you mean?"

"If you did this, wouldn't you do something to the car?"

I shrugged. "Yeah, most likely."

"They didn't."

"What're you thinking, Bear?"

"They didn't even slash a tire to stop us."

I said nothing. Bear's brain was processing this in parts. I wasn't sure where he was going with it.

"I half expected the car to blow up when I started it."

"But it didn't."

"Yeah, I know." He turned and crossed the porch.

I grabbed Jessie's hand and led her outside with my gun drawn. The passenger side of the car was shielded to the woods. I opened the back door for her and then ran around the front of the Tahoe and got in the front seat. I shifted into drive and drove down the gravel driveway in the dark.

"Lights?" Jessie asked.

"Not till we're on the road," I said. "Might be an ambush."

"They would have done it inside," Bear said.

I nodded. "I'm not taking any chances."

I eased onto the road and drove a half mile before turning on the headlights. I continued on to I-95 and took the northbound on-ramp.

Half an hour passed without a word being spoken.

"Jack?"

I looked over at Bear. He held his right arm tight to his chest.

"How's the shoulder?" I asked.

"Hurts. I think the stitches came out. It's bleeding."

I focused on the road ahead at a steady stream of cars in tight lines heading northeast into the rising sun. The sky changed from dark blue to light blue to purple and orange as the sun peeked up over the horizon. I soaked the sunrise in. The colors calmed my mind.

"What the hell is going on, Jack?"

I searched my mind for the answer.

"I've got no idea."

"All this, for beating up a couple damn CIA agents?"

"People are dying. We're being framed. It goes beyond that, Bear."

"They killed that family." He paused and looked out his window. "Dammit, we stopped them and they still killed that family. Little kids. The wife."

I said nothing. It had been on my mind the whole time. I felt responsible. Maybe Martinez had no intentions of hurting the family. But I stepped in and signed their death certificates in doing so.

"Maybe it's that simple," Bear said. "Maybe some other group killed the family 'cause they were afraid the family talked to us. Easy enough to pin on us."

The thought had crossed my mind already. But it was too simple, too clean. That would be easy to refute. "Doesn't explain Delaney and Abbot. There's something else going on here. Someone or some group behind this. And there's a damn reason. We're close to finding something out, and someone doesn't like that."

Bear leaned his seat back and crossed his left arm over his right. "What now?"

"I'm going to D.C."

"We should be there in what, five hours?"

"Not we. Just me."

"Like hell. I'm coming with you."

"Look at you. You'll weigh me down." I hated saying it. If I had to run, Bear would be a liability. "Besides, I need someone to watch over Jessie."

"Screw you, Jack."

15

I DROPPED BEAR AND JESSIE OFF AT A HOTEL IN PETERSBURG, VIRGINIA AND swapped the Tahoe for a rental car just outside of Richmond. It crossed my mind more than once that the Tahoe might have been bugged. It was risky driving the Tahoe as far as I did. But I figured whoever was after me had proved time and again that they would wait until I was settled somewhere before striking. Why would now be any different? Besides, I still wasn't sure that they followed us to Abbot's. The hit on Abbot could have been in motion long before he told us to come out to his lake house. That made sense. The hit had been planned before he talked to me. Otherwise, why not send a team and take all of us out?

I stopped at a convenience store and picked up a TracFone, then got back on I-95 northbound to Washington, D.C. The sedan provided a smoother ride than the Tahoe. I caught myself falling asleep more than once.

I exited the interstate in Springfield, Virginia and stopped at the first hotel I found. Paid cash for a two-night stay. The hotel wasn't fancy, a two story place with outside entrances to each room. I drove to the far end and walked up a flight of stairs to room 228. I ran the green programmed key card through the lock and the door clicked open. I stepped into the room. To my right was a bathroom. To the left a full length mirror followed by a shallow closet. A dresser with a TV on it leaned up against one wall. Across from the dresser was a queen-sized bed. On the far side of the bed was a round table with two chairs.

I pulled out the TracFone and the torn paper with Conners and the phone number missing one digit written on it. Blood stained the paper. Abbot's blood. My jaw clenched as anger built inside of me. I started dialing the number, stopping after the ninth digit. I tried to decide what number to press next. My finger hovered over the button labeled with the number five. Instead of pressing the button, I flipped the phone shut. Once I heard a voice on the other end of the line I'd need to act on whatever information it gave me. Right now I needed sleep. Sure, I'd been trained to operate in sleep-deprived situations, and I had been since leaving the little house in Iraq. But now I needed every bit of cohesion and clarity I could muster.

I took off my clothes and hung them over one of the chairs next to the table. Placed my gun on the nightstand and laid down. I was out within five minutes.

I awoke in a dark room. It took a few moments to remember my location and why I was there. I sat up and turned to look at the window. The sunlight that penetrated the folds of the drapes had disappeared. I pulled back the shades and saw that it was dark outside, too. I grabbed my watch. Seven p.m. I brushed off the initial burst of anger and took a deep breath. Seven hours of sleep would prove beneficial. A pen and pad of paper were placed next to my gun on the nightstand. I grabbed all three and moved to the table. My stomach growled. I leaned over and checked through the drapes. A Mexican restaurant next door caused my mouth to salivate.

I quickly dressed and left my room. Crossed the parking lot and entered the restaurant. I ordered take out and returned to the room to eat.

I picked up the pen and wrote Conners at the top of the notepad. Below that I wrote the nine digit number and below that I wrote the numbers zero through nine in order. My finger had hovered over five before I had lain down to sleep, so I decided to start with that one.

A raspy voice answered the phone midway through the first ring. "Hello?"

"Is this Conners?"

"Who's this?"

"This is, uh, a friend of the Colonel's."

"I know lots of Colonels. Which one?"

I took my chances. "The one who's dead now."

There was silence on the other end. Finally, the man spoke up. "Christ."

"First guess. What a surprise." After a pause I added, "I was in the house when he was murdered."

"OK, so you are who I think you are and I am who you think I am." He coughed. "We shouldn't say much else on the phone."

"Agreed. Where can I meet you?"

"Carlito's, it's a—do you know your way around the city?"

"Well enough."

"19th and I Street. You can't miss it."

"You sure—" I searched for the right words. "Listen, Conners. People are dying everywhere I go. I get the feeling I'm being framed. But, do you... is this place safe?"

"It is, and you are. Meet me at nine thirty tonight."

The line went dead. I flipped the phone shut and set it on the table. I stood and peeled back the curtains covering the window and studied the parking lot outside. The hotel's lot was motionless. A few cars came and went as families stumbled out of the restaurant and others made their way inside to take the place of those who had just left. The cycle of life, somewhat.

I wasn't sure about Conners. The cautious nature of our phone call and the reaction to Abbot's death made me think he was on my side, or a good actor. Aside from Bear, General Keller was the only other person I could trust. But I'd have to give Conners the benefit of the doubt. If the meeting turned out to be a double cross, I'd be ready.

I LEFT my car in the hotel parking lot and walked two blocks to the Metro station. I didn't want to risk losing the rental in the city if things went wrong. No one knew I was out here in Springfield, and I'd be happy letting them assume I stayed in the city somewhere. The train ride took half an hour. I got off at the Farragut West Metro Station. A few passengers exited the train before me. I followed them through the station, staying close to a group of two men and a woman. Took the stairs up and emerged at the corner of 17th and I Streets. I took a moment to get my bearings down. Across the street was the Farragut Park, a city block in length and half a city block in width. The park divided the north and southbound lanes of 17th Street.

I walked two blocks to the west, away from the park, and found Carlito's. The tinted windows of the restaurant made it impossible to see inside. I crossed the street and walked up to the entrance. A blue neon sign formed the image of a Martini glass with the restaurant's name next to it. I opened the door and stepped in. A man in a black suit and purple tie stood behind a wooden pulpit and asked for my name.

"I'm meeting someone."

"Name of the party you're meeting?"

I didn't answer. My eyes scanned the occupied tables in the restaurant. Eight couples, four families, a woman eating alone and in the back a single man. I walked toward the single man.

"Sir, you can't do that."

I looked over my shoulder. "I found him. It's all good." I continued walking, ignoring his protests.

The man at the table looked around the room. His head stopped when he saw me and his back straightened. He looked to be mid-fifties, maybe older. Short gray hair and a gray beard framed his face. He wore a blue sweater and tan slacks. He stood when I reached the table.

"Noble," he said.

"Conners."

I sat down on the padded leather bench seat across from him. A wood and glass partition separated us from the table behind me.

"Hungry?" He nodded at the waiter standing beside the table.

"Coffee," I said to the waiter.

Conners waited a moment then said, "Tell me from the beginning."

"I have a feeling you already know."

"That might be true, but I need to hear your version."

"Why don't you tell me your version?"

"We can go back and forth all night, Noble. But if you want my help you are going to start from the beginning."

"What kind of help can you provide me?"

"More than enough."

"You know where this leads?"

"I think I do."

"You think or you know?"

Conners sighed and shook his head. "You're not calling the shots here, Jack. Please, work with me."

I studied the man's face. His blue eyes didn't waver. He slightly tipped his head down and lifted his eyebrows. An outstretched arm and extended fingers reached toward me. He looked like he genuinely wanted to help. I didn't have much choice but to trust him, so I started from the beginning. I told him about the first six months in Iraq, shifting between different ops teams, each time given less and less responsibility. I told him about the family and Martinez's behavior and then recounted the scene in the street when Bear and I were mobbed by the group of Iraqi men.

"Wouldn't being attacked so close to the house be something that might have resulted in retaliation by you?" he asked.

"Why's that?"

"They were ready to kill you."

"No," I said. "They were defending their turf."

He shrugged and I continued telling him the events in order, as best as I remembered them. Occasionally he stopped me to ask a question or two, but for the most part he nodded as he listened to me rattle off the events of the last few days.

The waiter returned to the table with my cup of coffee while I was telling Conners about Abbot's murder. I had to stop mid-sentence. I dropped my voice to a scratch above a whisper after the waiter left.

He exhaled loudly after I gave him my version of Abbot's murder.

"Quite a story, Jack."

"It's more than a story."

"I know."

"Your turn. Spill."

He looked around the restaurant.

"I don't know how much I can tell. In here." He shrugged. "Now."

I said nothing and gave him a look that said he had better talk.

"Hey, aren't you worried about being spotted? Your damn picture was all over the TV and papers here."

"Stock photo of me in uniform." I ran my hand through my hair. "Doesn't look like me with this hair and beard."

Conners shrugged.

I waited for him to talk while he took a few bites of steak and washed it down with the amber beer in front of him.

I lit a cigarette.

"This is a non-smoking restaurant," he said through a mouthful of steak as he leaned forward and scanned the restaurant to make sure no one saw me light it, like a lookout in the boy's room in a high school.

"Don't care."

"OK," he put his fork and knife down on the edge of his plate, "I'll talk."

I waited.

"Delaney," he said. "He gave you something, right?"

I nodded, didn't say anything.

"Did he tell you where to go next?"

"A bullet stopped him."

"Not yours, right?"

I cocked my head and didn't answer.

"Right, I know. OK, so...Delaney, he gave you a, uh, something that leads to something else." He lifted an eyebrow, waiting for a response.

I nodded.

"Only you don't know where to take what he gave you?"

I waited for him to continue. When he didn't, I responded, "That's right. That's what I told you a few minutes ago."

"OK, OK, Jack. I'm just making sure—"

"Cut the crap, Conners. For all we know someone is twenty minutes behind me and is going to open fire in here in a few minutes."

A couple of diners stopped mid-conversation and looked at me.

I smiled and waved.

"We're actors. Just rehearsing lines."

They shook their heads and returned to their conversations.

"Dammit, Jack. Calm down. Let me be thorough."

I'd grown tired of thorough. I wanted names. I wanted reasons. None of this 'confirm you did this and that' crap he kept feeding me.

"Greyhound," he said.

"The bus line?"

"Yes, the key goes to a locker at the Greyhound station."

"What's there?"

Conners clenched his jaw. Thick muscles worked in back and he pursed his lips together. "I don't know for sure."

"Who's there?"

"Don't know that either."

"Did you work with Delaney?"

"Yes."

"Who do you work for?"

"Can't tell you that."

I took a sip of coffee. "Why can't you tell me?"

"Because, officially, we don't exist." He waved his hands in the air, partly to be demonstrative and partly to waft the smoke away. "Officially, I don't exist."

I nodded while keeping my eyes focused on his. It wasn't out of the realm of possibility. Even within the known agencies there were departments that didn't exist. I was attached to one of them. There were also men who didn't exist, men who were worse than Martinez. Men who did things that people refused to acknowledge could be done in the name of freedom. The things that had to be done to defend that freedom. Nobody wants to think of what actions must be performed to keep them safe.

"Sounds like a cushy position."

"Jack, you get those documents and call me. I need to take a look at them and then we can figure this out."

"What's the locker number?"

He shook his head and looked to the side.

"B915."

I reached into my pocket, pulled out the key and tossed it at him.

"Here, you go get it yourself then."

He pushed the keys back to me.

"Don't be stupid. One call and you're locked up for life."

I narrowed my eyes and stared him down for fifteen seconds.

"That's what this comes down to?"

He slumped over and placed his elbows on the table.

"I'm sorry, Jack. That was uncalled for."

I said nothing.

"I know where this goes. Most of it at least. And if I go get those documents, and someone is waiting, I'm a dead man. Look at me." He waved his hands in front of his body. "If I die, then all knowledge of this dies. And you'll most likely die. As a traitor, too."

"And if I go there and someone is waiting?"

"You got more than a fifty-fifty chance to take them out."

I sat back and crossed my arms. There weren't many possible scenarios, but each one that existed played through my mind. The best option was for me to go to the Greyhound station and retrieve whatever sat inside the locker. I reached across the table and grabbed the key. Slid across the bench and stood next to the table.

"I'll call you in a few hours."

"I'll be waiting."

I turned and started to walk away.

"Jack," he said.

I looked over my shoulder.

"Like I said, I know where this goes. If you decide to open those documents, you need to prepare yourself for what's in there."

I walked back to the table.

"Where is that?"

Conners shook his head. "I can't tell you. Not until I know you are one hundred percent on my side."

"You haven't figured out that I am?"

"No. Once you return, I'll know, though."

16

THE D.C. GREYHOUND STATION WAS LOCATED ON 1ST STREET, ABOUT TWO and a half miles from the restaurant. I decided to walk. I went a block north to K Street then headed east until I reached 1st Street. I figured the later I arrived at the station the better. Chances were the schedule thinned out at night, resulting in fewer people around.

A cold wind blew down the street, numbing my face and carrying a combination of wood smoke and exhaust fumes. The sky clouded over. It looked as if a spring snowstorm was brewing.

My watch read 11:30 when I reached the Greyhound station. I walked up 1st Street and turned on L Street. Continued past the bus station and stopped. A tree in bloom provided cover from the evenly spaced black wrought iron lamp posts that lined the sidewalk. I leaned against the tree and scanned the area. The activity across the street was virtually nil, with only a few people here and there. A red four-door sedan pulled up and dropped off a young woman, late teens or early twenties, probably heading back to college after her spring break.

I scanned the parking lot behind me and didn't see anything out of the ordinary. There were only a dozen or so cars, all parked close to the lights. They belonged to employees, I figured. There was nothing that resembled a government official's car.

I pushed off the tree and walked across the street. The area behind the glass double-door entrance was empty. I pulled the door open and stepped into the yellow tinted bus station. Directly in front of me was a large board displaying a digital schedule. To the left was a bank of windows. Ropes stretched out and across, creating a maze for passengers to wait in before buying their tickets. No one was in line. Only one window was occupied by an overweight lady reading a book. She looked up and then quickly back down when I made eye contact with her.

To my right were several rows of seats in a blue and white checkerboard pattern. I turned and headed that way. The outside facing wall was blank, painted a drab brown. The back wall was lined with lockers, as was the area to the left of the seats. The place was filled with row upon row of gray and blue and green painted lockers.

Only six seats were occupied, consisting of two couples and two individual travelers. None took note of me. I walked down the aisle in the middle of the seating area and took a seat at the last row. Then I watched and waited.

I let an hour pass. I did nothing. I talked to no one. I let my eyes wander to the row of lockers and focused on row B. No one entered. No one exited. Nice and quiet. Part of me felt it was too quiet. Could I trust Conners? If he wanted me to go down, this was the perfect set up. I was trapped here. A tactical team would have no trouble extracting me, dead or alive. I brushed the thought aside. He could have had me taken care of outside the restaurant. The way I saw it, he wanted to get his hands on these documents as much as I did. If he planned on taking me down, he'd do it after I handed them over to him. The simple solution was to not hand them over.

I got up and went outside, stopped near the glass doors and watched the sparse traffic as it passed. A car drove through the loop that ran in front of the building. It slowed near the entrance, but never stopped. Tinted windows blocked any view inside of the car.

I took a deep breath before walking back inside. The cold air cleansed my lungs. I headed toward the rows of lockers and turned at the row labeled B and walked past locker B915. I stopped ten feet away and looked over my shoulder. No one followed me. I cut down a cross aisle and turned at row L where I grabbed the key out of a random locker. If I needed to stash anything, I'd do it in that locker. Probably the last place they would look.

I went back to row B, peeking around the corner to make sure no one was waiting by locker B915. Satisfied that the row was empty, I walked up to the locker. I stood there for a few minutes, key in hand, debating whether or not to open it. I couldn't shake the feeling that I was being set up. I didn't know Conners well enough to put double crossing me past him. Hell, it didn't even have to be him. It could be any number of people I'd apparently pissed off recently.

I took a deep breath, exhaled and stuck the key in the locker. Turned it and opened the rectangular metal door. It squeaked against its hinges. Inside sat a black bag with a zipper on top and a mesh back. I grabbed the bag and turned away from the front of the bus station. I walked down the aisle until it opened up into an empty seating area.

This time I sat in the first row of seats. I pulled my jacket open, clearing a path to my Beretta. My heart beat fast and my breath quickened. The training I had been put through taught me how to control panic. I followed the steps and relaxed myself to the point where I could focus.

I unzipped the bag and looked up.

Two men stood fifteen feet away from me. Two men, that upon second glance, I knew.

"Jack Noble."

I nodded while zipping the bag shut.

"Gallo, Bealle."

Gallo stepped forward. A towel hung over his hand, a weak attempt at hiding his weapon. He smiled when my gaze lifted from the gun to meet his eyes. "Let's go, Jack."

BEALLE WALKED in front of me. Gallo behind, his gun pressed into my back. I held the bag tight to my chest. For some reason they didn't try to take it, at least not yet.

We stepped through the front door and the wind hit like a wall of ice. The sweat on my forehead evaporated and gave me a slight chill.

They led me down L Street to an empty parking lot. We moved to the middle of the dirt and gravel lot, stopping outside the range of the street lights.

"We're not here to hurt you," Gallo said.

"What's the gun for then?"

"Our protection."

I said nothing and kept the bag secure in my arms.

"We aren't too keen on taking you on again, especially after what you've been through."

"How'd you know I'd be here?"

"We have sources," Bealle said.

"Conners?"

"No. I don't know any Conners."

"Me either," Gallo said. "Let's go someplace we can sit down and talk."

I wondered if that was for their protection as well.

We walked through the streets of Washington, D.C. until we found a twenty-four hour diner. Gallo asked for the booth in the corner by the window. He sat against the wall. I sat with my back to the restaurant and Bealle squeezed in next to me. I placed the bag between my left leg and the window.

A brown-haired waitress came to our table. I ordered coffee. Gallo and Bealle ordered water.

"What do you know, Jack?" Gallo asked.

I shrugged. "Not much. I know that you guys framed me for the murder of that Iraqi family—"

"That wasn't us, Jack." Gallo placed his elbows on the table. He leaned forward. "Martinez was pissed. He probably still is. You made him look bad and then kicked his ass. He's a hothead. But it's not like him to go back, murder a family and then frame you."

"What were we doing there that night?" I asked. "Were we there to kill the man?"

Gallo glanced at Bealle and nodded.

"Yes," Bealle said. "If he didn't give up the information he was to be terminated."

"What about the woman?"

"No, that wasn't part of it."

"Martinez took that too far," Gallo said. "That's something we agree on. But, you know, there are no rules, man. We're hunting out there and we need to get the information and neutralize the threat before it gets too far."

"And that's where you screwed up, Jack," Bealle said. "Repeatedly, you've gotten in our way. Not just us, but other teams."

"It's because I can't work like that. I'm not some security detail. For eight years I've worked on these teams and always been involved. Now we go to Iraq after the attacks and I'm standing in doorways and providing the muscle. Hell with that."

I leaned back in my seat and crossed my arms over my chest and looked out the window at drunken people pouring out of a bar. I checked my watch and saw that it was now two a.m.

Gallo took a moment and responded. "It's not just you. Other teams in the co-op are having this issue as well."

I hiked my shoulders and held out my hands in a *'who-cares?'* gesture.

"What else do you know?" Gallo asked.

"I know that half the people who come in contact with me end up dead. Stick around and you might skew that ratio even further."

Gallo smiled.

"I know that somehow they tracked me. I figured they used the cell phone and got rid of it. Still, Abbot was killed." I locked eyes with Gallo. "They murdered him and left me alone. So tell me, what the hell is going on here?"

Gallo took a drink of water and leaned back. "There were six teams. You know that, you were there with us. Six teams, a dozen Marines." He turned and looked at the window at the crowd of people passing by, laughing and talking with each other. "Four are dead, six are in prison on base and you and Logan are on the run."

The gravity of the situation hit home. I opened my mouth to speak. Nothing came out.

"You see where this is going?"

"What are they in prison for?"

"Returning to the scene of an interrogation and murdering any Iraqis there."

I felt sick. "Why didn't—why didn't Abbot tell me this?" My mind raced as the world closed in. "He was about to. He had to make a call for my next contact, but he was going to tell me this before I left."

Gallo shrugged and shook his head.

"What did you tell them when they asked about the family?" I asked.

"They never did," Bealle said. "At least, they never asked us. Who knows if they asked Martinez?"

"Where is Martinez?"

"We haven't seen him since that night. Word is he took leave and came back..."

"Here," I said. "He's in D.C."

Gallo nodded and continued. "We never filed a complaint, signed a statement, nothing against you or Logan. And the other teams we've spoken with said the same. But..."

"But?" I hung on his words and watched as his face twisted in thought.

"There was always a team that didn't have, uh, Marines attached. Six CIA agents, that's it. I don't mean us. Martinez and five agents."

I knew where this was heading.

"We never worked with Martinez until a few months ago."

"When they reorganized the teams," I said.

Gallo nodded and continued. "Well, can you guess who took over the other five teams?"

"I'm guessing the other five men who worked on the CIA only team." I said.

"Yup," Bealle said.

I turned in the seat and leaned back against the glass so I could see both of them. I didn't care who was outside. If someone was going to take me out, let them do it.

"Someone is trying to take apart the program then," I said.

Both men nodded.

"That's what we think," Gallo said.

"Any ideas who?"

"We've been trying to determine that. Doing our own investigation. We can't find anyone who knows. It's coming from high up, whether in our agency or outside of it, it's high up."

I thought about it for a second before responding. "So why not just terminate the program? Send us back to the Marines to finish our careers behind a desk and merge your teams together. That would make more sense, right?"

"Absolutely," Gallo said. "Why wouldn't they do that? That's what we can't figure out."

"Because someone else high up is pushing to keep the program going."

Gallo shrugged. "Makes sense."

"Another question, then. So we're saying that someone wanted us out of the way. Any ideas why?"

"So we can act however they want us to. There were too many incidents like yours where a Marine got in the way."

"You say that like we're some damn choir boys."

Both men laughed.

"It also makes me question what they were going to do once we were out of the way."

Gallo nodded. "Yeah, I wonder too. I think I have an answer, but I don't want to believe it."

I held out my hands. "Might as well."

Gallo opened his mouth to speak, but didn't.

Bealle said, "I think you know where he's going with that, Jack. Let's not go down that road. Right now we just want to put a stop to what's going on."

"What do you care?"

"We might not agree with the new direction. And if that's the case, we might be terminated also."

We said nothing for five minutes. The three of us sat in silence. I went over the conversation, making an extra mental note of the most important parts. I hoped that whatever was in the folder in the black bag could shed some light on what they said.

Gallo slid out of his seat and stood in front of the table. "Jack, we're going to leave you for now."

Bealle placed a piece of paper in front of me. "Those are our numbers. Call in the morning and we'll meet up. Give you some time to absorb this. Think it over. Maybe something will click."

With that, they left. I got up and switched seats so my back was against the wall, giving me a view of the diner. I watched Bealle and Gallo leave, keeping my eye on them until they turned out of sight. I had to shake my head as I looked around the diner. How had I missed so many people entering?

When the waitress came by, I ordered another cup of coffee. A few minutes later she returned and set the coffee down in front of me. I declined when she asked if I needed anything else. I watched her walk back to the wait station, and then I pulled the black bag onto my lap and unzipped it. I slid the manila folder out of the bag and set it on the table. My thumb and forefinger wrapped around the outer corner of the folder. I took a deep breath and opened it.

I didn't know exactly what to expect, but my initial reaction was disappointment. There were just a few papers inside and nothing else. I turned the papers over and read the first line.

Then I read it again.

"Holy shit," I said out loud, garnering more than a few looks from the resident bar-goers in my presence.

There, on the first line of the first document was the name Robert Marlowe, Deputy Secretary of Defense, a man who had a vested interest in the situation in Iraq for sure.

17

THE LIST OF NAMES ON THE PAPER INCLUDED SEVERAL THAT I DIDN'T KNOW. Marlowe was the most damning. I recognized a few other politicians as well as some of the upper brass of the Armed Forces. The best plan of action was to confront Marlowe. And that's why I stood across the street from his house at four in the morning.

Marlowe's house was an end unit on a block of row homes. The houses were recently built and designed to look two hundred years old.

The quiet tree-lined block offered enough cover for me to watch the house from the street. So I did. I leaned back against a tree and staked out his house for half an hour. I watched for movement. Saw none. I crossed the street, walked past his house and turned right on the cross street. This led me along the side of his house. I looked to the side. All three windows were black.

An alley cut behind the row homes, separating their backyards from the homes on the next street. The alley was wide enough for a garbage truck to fit through, plus a few feet on either side. Dotted along the alley were blue plastic trash bins, each pushed up against a continuous six foot wooden privacy fence.

I pressed back against Marlowe's fence and waited five minutes. The stillness of the morning allowed me to hear anything that moved, which amounted to nothing more than a cat.

I pulled myself up on the fence and threw my leg over. A breeze blew by, warmer and thicker with humidity than what I'd felt during the past day. I looked up at the sky. The moon hung high directly above. To the west a thick line of dark clouds approached. I couldn't help but think how convenient the trashcan and impending spring storm were. If I needed to dispose of a body, this would be the day.

I crouched and moved to the back outer corner of the fence. Again, I watched the house for any signs of life inside. The windows promised darkness behind the brick and pale vinyl siding.

I reached into my jacket pockets and pulled out the thin gloves I purchased on the walk over. I put the gloves on and cut across the yard, my back against the fence. I made my way to the house in the same manner, avoiding the area beyond the shadowy cover the fence provided. Before I made my way to the back door, I lightly tapped one of the windows. If Marlowe had a dog, that should be enough to rouse him.

I waited, then tapped again and was met with silence.

Four steps led up to the back door. I took them from the side. Kept my back pressed against the house. I cracked the glass storm door and grabbed the doorknob. It turned. I couldn't believe it, an unlocked door in the middle of D.C. Was Marlowe really that stupid? I decided not to debate Marlowe's intelligence and instead gently pushed the door and slipped through the opening. I held my breath while waiting for an alarm to go off. I had thought about cutting the phone wires while outside, but I figured if Marlowe had a security system installed, it would be independent of the phone system and would likely detect my attempt to foil it.

The alarm didn't go off. At least not that I could tell. Maybe it was a silent alarm and was notifying the police at that very moment. Hell, maybe it was something the Department had installed, and they were en route. That actually made sense. If that were the case this would end badly. If I got caught here it would result in more than a simple breaking and entering. But had I really committed B&E? The damn door was unlocked. I planned to point that out to Marlowe.

I shook my head to clear the thoughts and continued through the house. I stood just inside the back door in the great room. It was plainly decorated with two couches and a simple wooden table between them. Two stacks of books sat on the middle of the table. I didn't see a TV or stereo. I moved through the living area of the great room and past the dining room, which had a round glass table with four black chairs.

I walked to the door located at the far end of the room. It had no handle. I pushed it. It swung open, revealing the kitchen. A light was on above the stove. It was dim, but provided enough illumination to see the room. I heard a click and my eyes moved to the source of the sound. A coffee pot had turned on. A moment later percolating sounds promising fresh coffee filled the kitchen.

It wouldn't be long till Marlowe pushed through the kitchen door. I stood next to it, back against the wall. The open door would block his view of me, giving me the element of surprise.

A few minutes later I heard the rush of water from above. Marlowe, or someone in the house, had started a shower. Ten minutes later the thumping of footsteps coming down the wooden stairs echoed through the house. I squeezed my gun and pressed even harder against the wall.

The door pushed open with a knock, coming within inches of hitting me. It swung back shut and Marlowe, dressed in gray slacks and an untucked white t-shirt, shuffled toward the coffee maker. He opened a cabinet door and pulled down a blue or black mug with a golden seal of some sort on it.

"Grab one for me, too."

He froze for a moment. Set the mug down and grabbed another. He turned around and looked at me with a blank expression.

"Noble," he said. "Jack Noble, right?"

I nodded. Said nothing.

"I thought I saw you a couple days ago down by the National Mall."

I shrugged and decided not to respond. I wanted to see how far he would go on his own.

He cleared his throat. "Mind if I fill these for us?" He turned without waiting for a response from me and filled the two mugs three quarters of the way full. He grabbed both by their handles and started toward me. "Why don't we sit, Jack?"

I moved in front of the door and nodded to the table in the back corner of the kitchen.

He went to the table, set the coffee down and took a seat in the corner.

I remained standing.

"I know why you're here," he said. "Let me start by telling you that I—"

"Shut up."

He pursed his lips and sat back in his chair. Crossed one leg over the other and placed his hands flat on the table.

"How do you know me?"

"From the TV. You were on the news wanted in connection with that man, what's his name? Oh, yeah. Delaney."

"Don't bullshit me, Marlowe." I pulled out a chair and sat across from him. I placed my hand on the table and kept the gun trained on him. "You said you recognized me in the city. I was eating lunch outside. You walked by with two other politicians and a couple of agents assigned to you. One of them eyed me as you all passed by."

He shrugged. "Yeah, I saw you. Like I said I recog—"

"That was before I had met with Delaney."

He looked down at the table and shifted in his seat.

"So you better cut the crap and answer my question."

He lifted his mug to his lips and took a sip while reaching one hand under the table.

I lifted the gun. "Stop right there."

"I'm just getting a pack of cigarettes out," he said as he lifted his hand up, a cardboard box held between his thumb and forefinger. He offered me one and I declined, so he stuffed the pack back in his pocket.

I settled back in my chair and watched as he looked between me and the ceiling.

"Your name's Jack Noble. You're a Sergeant in the U.S. Marine Corps. But that doesn't matter. Your jacket says that you're a Sniper. But that doesn't matter, either. In fact, there might be one or two snipers who have never even heard of you and that's simply because of your boot camp legend." He stopped, tipped his head and stared me in the eye. "Eight weeks through recruit training you were optioned for a special joint program sponsored by the CIA in which you were essentially loaned out to become part of an Ops team. On the Marine side you had General Keller and Colonel Abbot running things. On the CIA side, well, that's classified. If you know the names then you do. If not, I'm not at liberty to say them."

He stopped and nodded with his eyebrows hiked. I waited for him to continue, but he didn't say anything else.

"How do you know all this?" I said.

He crossed his arms and held his head cocked slightly to the side.

"If you're stalling because someone is on the way, know that I will kill you before they take me down. As it stands right now I'm wanted on four counts in Iraq and at least two here. One more isn't going make a damn bit of difference to me."

Marlowe smiled. A single chuckle muffled itself in his throat.

I stood and kicked my chair back behind me. I stretched out my arm, pointing the gun at his head. "Do you think I'm screwing around, Marlowe?"

He remained calm, lifting his hands and gesturing me to sit down.

I regained my composure, grabbed the chair and sat back down.

"Jack, I know all of this because it's my job to know. It's my program. I started it. I got the funding. I put the principal parties into place. They reported, ultimately, to me. Every month we would meet and discuss the operations. You were in the first group. First successful group, that is. Of course, you already know that. Your group turned out to be exactly what we wanted and proved that the program would be a success." He gave me a slight nod. "Then the world went to hell in a hand basket because of that damn Bin Laden. Outside pressure forced us to turn our attention to Afghanistan and Pakistan."

"I was sent to Iraq."

He brought the mug to his mouth and sipped loudly.

"I was against that."

"Against it? You run the program, right? That's what you just said. Plus, Iraq is your policy. Damn man, I've read about you before. You've been pushing to get in there since the attacks."

He smiled and shook his head. "Things don't work that way, son. What I say is dictated by someone above me."

"How far above you?"

"I..." He paused. "I'm not going to answer that, Jack. Besides, that isn't what you came here to discuss. Is it?"

I nodded and said nothing. He had a point. I really didn't care who ordered me to Iraq. I wanted to know who set me up and who killed Delaney and Abbot.

"So back to the program." He reached for his inside pocket again, but changed his mind. "There was some dissension right away when we split the groups, especially when the roles of the operations were defined."

"You mean like me and Logan guarding doors."

He nodded and continued. "That was just scratching the surface though. Some people started to have an interest in shutting the program down."

"You," I said.

He narrowed his eyes at me. "Why do you think that?"

I opened my jacket and pulled the documents from inside my coat pocket and tossed them on the table.

Marlowe picked them up and studied them for a moment and then set them down. "What do you think this has to do with anything?"

"I'm not sure, but two people died so I could get those, so they must mean something."

He lifted his chin and exhaled loudly. "They do, but it's not what you think."

Through the window I could see the sky turning a pale blue in advance of the rising sun. Time was running out. I had to choose between the documents and the program. "Tell me this, then. Are you the one behind terminating the program?"

"Yes, Jack. But not in the way you think."

"Explain."

"I know where this operation is heading, and I don't want to be responsible for it. I wanted to terminate the Middle East operations and reassign everyone. Unfortunately, certain people had too much to lose by me doing so. On the flip side, certain people had a lot to gain by me doing so. My stance deepened the divide, and not just between the agency and the Marines. In the past week a damn civil war broke out between everyone." He clasped his hands behind his head and exhaled. "When I saw you, I thought you were sent to kill me. When things fell in place the way they did, I knew that wasn't the case."

I ran my hands across my face and through my hair while processing the information. "Four Marines are dead. Six are in prison. Two are on the run in the U.S."

"Yeah, I know."

"Who in the CIA is responsible for that?"

He shook his head and looked down at the table. "It's not the CIA, Jack. We've been watching them the entire time."

My head started to spin. It couldn't be. Could it? "Abbot," I said under my breath. I looked up expecting to see a look of confirmation.

"No. It's true that Abbot didn't want you guys over there. But the program benefited him. Plus, he wouldn't want you guys killed."

I thought back to the Audi A8. The flat screen TV in the lake house, at a time when most people still had tube TVs. *The program benefited him.*

"Then who, Marlowe? I don't have all day. Just get to it, and I'll handle it."

"Who's left, Jack?"

I knew. I knew before he said it. It had always been there. "General Keller." I said it flatly.

Marlowe nodded. "I can't say with one hundred percent certainty how, but yes, Keller is who I suspect."

"So why didn't you act on it?"

He placed his forearm in front of him on the table and leaned over it. He rubbed his chin with his hand. "I've got too much to lose, Jack. Ultimately, whatever happens with the program and those in it, we'd just sweep it under the rug. No one worse for wear in knowing. Understand? If I come out and accuse a General of this..." He straightened up. "Hell, that would be political suicide, and I'm not willing to take that risk."

I said nothing. I understood what he was saying. I didn't agree, but I saw his point.

"I'd sure as hell like to know why, though. He turned on his own damn men."

"He never liked the program," I said under my breath.

"How's that?"

"He never liked the program," I repeated. "I remember sitting in his office when I was nothing but a recruit. He was sending us off. He hated it. But he had no choice." I lifted my eyes and met Marlowe's stare. "And now he's trying to end the program, permanently. Abbot knew what he was up to. He was going to tell me. Keller had him killed. He didn't know we were there though. I didn't answer his call."

Marlowe hiked his shoulders and held out his hand while his lips formed a frown.

"Anything else?" I asked.

"I'm afraid I've said too much already, Jack."

I sat back and studied his face. He had more to tell me. I could see it in his eyes. I glanced at my watch. It was almost six a.m. I had to go, get back to the hotel in Springfield and get my car. I stood and turned to leave.

"Jack?"

I looked over my shoulder.

"It should go without saying that I never shared this information with you."

I nodded, turned to face him and grabbed the documents off the table. "I'll be taking these since you already know what they are."

He started to stand in protest, but backed down when I turned my gun toward him. "Take it, Jack. It really means nothing to you."

"We should play poker sometime, Marlowe. You're horrible at bluffing." I pushed the door open and stopped again. "I'm going after Keller. I'll be back if your story doesn't jive."

18

I FOUND A TAXI WILLING TO TAKE ME TO SPRINGFIELD. FIGURED THAT WOULD be better than dealing with crowded Metro stations. The driver fought the traffic and dropped me off two blocks from the hotel. I walked the remaining distance. There wasn't anything of value in the room, so I didn't go in. I got in the car and merged onto I-95 southbound. Along the way I called Conners and told him I had to act on a lead and I'd get in touch with him as soon as I knew something.

Two hours later I arrived in Petersburg and parked a block away from the hotel where Jessie and Bear were staying.

I wanted Bear to come with me to Keller's. He could provide backup, even if he wasn't in the room during the confrontation. I still didn't trust Marlowe, and something told me Keller would be expecting me. I thought about taking this to one of my agency contacts, but knew that would get me nowhere. For one, the guys I knew could care less about political BS. They would wave me off and tell me to go piss up a tree. Regular authorities were out of the question. They'd arrest me without giving it a second thought. Hell, I probably had a shoot-on-sight designation on me by that point.

There was still the question of who Delaney and Conners worked for, and who pulled the trigger on Abbot. I hoped Keller could answer those questions for me.

I got out of the rental car and walked to the hotel. I kept my head down and wore sunglasses. Cars passed by at regular intervals, but no one seemed to care about the guy walking on the sidewalk while they were busying themselves driving to work.

The distance between D.C. and Petersburg, Virginia was approximately 120 miles. That made the difference in temperature even more astounding. At nine a.m. it was warm enough here for me to want to take off my jacket. I kept it on to keep my weapon concealed, but I started to sweat under its bulk.

I reached the hotel and scanned the parking lot before entering the lobby. A young lady stood behind the counter. She glanced up at me, smiled, and then returned to her keyboard when she saw that I had no intention of approaching her.

An elderly woman stood alone in the elevator lobby. I stopped next to her and waited for the elevator doors to open. A minute passed. I glanced around and saw that the elevator call button had not been pushed. I looked at her, smiled and leaned forward to press the single button with an up arrow printed on it. A chime sounded and the doors opened. I stuck one hand in the opening and gestured her through.

"Three please," she said.

I had already pressed the button for the third floor. That's where Bear and Jessie were staying.

Less than half a minute later the doors opened and I waited for the woman to exit. She did so and turned to the right. I stepped out and turned left.

The room was located at the end of the hall. I jogged to the door. I wanted to tell Bear everything I had learned in D.C.

And I wanted to kiss Jessie.

I stood in front of the door and rapped on it with my knuckles. A pinhead of light shone through the peephole cut into the center of the door. A few heavy steps rumbled below my feet and the pinhead of light disappeared. A second later the door opened.

"Jack," Bear said.

I nodded and stepped through the open doorway as he walked to the back of the room. I looked around, but didn't see Jess. My eyes met Bear's. He wore my disappointment on his face.

"She's gone."

"Where'd she go?"

"Don't know. I woke up and she was gone." He opened a dresser drawer and pulled out an envelope. "She left this for you."

I took the envelope labeled "Jack" from him and stared at it for a minute. "You read it?"

"Nah."

"She give any indication she was leaving?"

Bear shook his head and hiked his shoulders up an inch.

"You're sure she left. She wasn't taken?"

"Jack, no, man. We went to sleep. I got up and she was gone. If someone was going to go through the trouble of taking her from the room, don't you think they would have killed me?"

I fell back on the bed and stared at the ceiling. He had a point. If someone had broken in, they would have either taken him with them or taken him out. Plus, Bear would have woken up if someone broke in. The man might be nicknamed Bear and look like a bear, but he sure as hell didn't sleep like one.

"Read the letter, Jack."

I lifted my arms and held the envelope over my face. I decided against opening it, at least for a while. We had work to do. I sat up and tucked the sealed letter into one of the inside pockets of my jacket.

"I'll read it later," I said. "I need to catch you up on what's happened."

I talked, and Bear listened. He remained silent until I finished.

After I was done, he said, "You're sure Keller is behind it?"

I took a moment to respond. "I don't know, Bear. But I'm going to find out."

He nodded and leaned back in his chair.

"What I need to know is if you think you can come with me. Can you?"

"Yeah, Jack. I'm good to go. It hurts, but it won't stop me if things go south."

We sat in silence the next few minutes.

Bear leaned forward, his mouth open an inch. He furrowed his eyebrows and pointed at the TV behind me. "Where's the remote?" He got up.

I turned in my seat and saw what had shocked him.

Bear picked up the remote and unmuted the station.

The display under the woman said her name was Cassandra Phillips. She spoke in the serious tone all newscasters had to perfect.

"Once again, we are stunned and shocked to be reporting this breaking news. At six a.m. this morning, police found the bodies of Richard Gallo and Eddie Bealle, both CIA agents involved in the conflict in Afghanistan. The reports we've received indicate that the men were murdered, execution style, in downtown Washington, D.C."

They flashed head shots of both men on the screen and then cut to a scene in front of Gallo's home. A local news team spoke to his wife, who kept herself half hidden behind the door. A small child with blond hair clung to her exposed leg.

I tuned out the broadcast and turned to Bear.

"I just met with them last night."

"That's what you said."

"Someone is going to recall seeing them with me."

"You didn't do it, right Jack?"

Cassandra's voice returned on the TV and I spun around to watch.

"There are no suspects in the case at this time. Police have said they are looking for a person of interest, but details have not been released. We will keep you apprised of the story as we become aware of additional developments."

I threw my hands behind my head and grabbed my hair. "It's either the same people that took out Delaney, or it's..."

Bear waited a second and then prompted me to speak.

"Martinez," I said.

"Martinez? You think he'd take out his own guys?"

"They weren't his guys. He was loyal to his original team. So, yeah, I wouldn't put this past him."

Bear turned off the TV and moved to the window. He pulled back the curtains and studied the parking lot.

"We should go."

I got up and walked to the door.

"Yeah. Get your stuff."

———

WE HURRIED down the block and got in the car. The hotel was five minutes from the interstate. I stopped and filled up on gas, and then hit the interstate heading south. We drove in silence until we crossed the North Carolina state border.

"It's a good six hours to Savannah, so catch up on sleep if you need to," I said.

Bear said nothing. He stared out the window. His elbow propped on the door sticking out the open window.

I reached inside my jacket and traced the edges of the envelope Jessie left me. I wondered what the letter said. Probably the same things she said five years ago when we split up for good. Although, for good didn't mean forever. She even told me that. And I thought that maybe for good ended now. Apparently not, though. I needed to talk to her. To find out if it would make a difference if I left the military and became a cop or a firefighter or anything other than what I was now.

"Did she say anything?" I asked.

"Who?"

"Jessie. Did she say anything at all that gave you any indication she was leaving?"

"Nah. She just slipped out in the middle of the night."

I turned the wheel, adjusting to the curve in the road and said nothing.

"Maybe once we're done you should go back to Virginia."

"Think she went home?"

Bear shook his head. "After what's happened? I doubt it, man. She probably got on a bus, went to the airport and picked a destination."

"That's how she ended up in Virginia."

"I remember, Jack."

1 9

General Keller lived halfway between Parris Island, South Carolina and Savannah, Georgia in a housing development near Hilton Head where the homes cost half a million dollars. It raised some eyebrows when he bought it, but there were rumors that his wife had penned a series of romantic suspense novels and nailed down a seven figure advance from a major publisher. Still, for the regular working man it was tough to see your superior living in a McMansion and driving around a ninety thousand dollar Mercedes.

It didn't take a math whiz to put two and two together. Abbot and his new Audi A8 and decked out weekend home. Keller with his oversized house and overpriced Mercedes. They got it all from kickbacks. Blood money.

We pulled into the half-constructed neighborhood and turned away from the dirt-packed street where the wooden framed skeletons of houses lined the road. Bear leaned back in his seat and did his best to stay out of sight. I turned on Keller's road and eased past his house, taking in as much of the yellow stucco two story house as I could in the few seconds it took to pass. We'd been inside the house the previous summer for a housewarming party he threw a few months after he moved in. I searched my mind for a map of the layout of the house, but couldn't recall it all. The house was big. That's all I remembered.

The street looped around and connected with the main road. I turned left and then left again on Keller's street and parked the car three houses down from his. There was a curve in the road that gave us a decent view of the front of the house. Keller's black full-sized Mercedes was parked in the driveway, and a Jeep Wrangler with tires stained orange from mud was parked on the street in front of the house.

"He's got guests," Bear said.

"We can wait a bit," I said.

"What if they don't leave?"

"Then we deal with them."

"Jack?"

I shifted in my seat to look at Bear. "Yeah?"

"What if—" he paused and ran a hand across his face. "What if Marlowe lied?"

"You mean what if Keller wasn't involved?"

"Well, that, yeah. But also, what if he set you up? Set us up?"

I nodded slowly, letting my eyes shift toward the front of the house. "I thought about that, Bear. I did. Here's the way I see it. Marlowe gave up Keller without directly saying his name. He led me to figure it out, meaning one of two things. Marlowe is as deep in this as Keller, and I don't doubt that for one minute, but it's just what side of it he's on. He's for the program, but not the way it's being run. In that case, he knows Keller's involvement with what's happened to us and the other teams. He can't say anything for political reasons—"

"Or maybe Keller has something on Marlowe."

"Yeah, maybe Keller does have something on Marlowe and if he came out and accused Keller, it would be political suicide. Maybe even more than that. With all that's happened, jail time could be involved. None of us could be considered a choir boy. Top to bottom."

Bear nodded and said nothing.

"Or, yeah, maybe they are working together. Sent us down here so they could finish what they started in Iraq. We could walk into that house and be shot on sight."

After a minute Bear asked, "What's your gut tell you?"

I thought it over.

"My gut tells me that Marlowe is on our side, at least, as much as he can be. That Keller was the architect behind this plan and somehow Abbot was involved. Whether he was for or against is anybody's guess. I think he was going to blow the whistle the other night before he was murdered. But, whether Marlowe lied or not, I fully expect Keller to be ready for me when I knock on that door. They've been a step ahead the whole time it seems."

"Yeah. Wait. You're going to knock on the door?"

"I want you to wait outside, Bear. You're going to wait in the car while I go inside. After five minutes, move to the house."

"I'm going to look like a damn peepin' Tom out here."

I laughed, the reaction caused by nerves more than anything. "We're waiting till sunset." I pointed at the wide orange sun hovering over the houses at the end of the street. "Another half hour and it should be dark out here."

Bear nodded.

"You remember the layout of the house?"

"A bit," I said. "Walk into a ten by ten foyer. Stairs off to the left, beyond that a dining room. On the right, the foyer opens up to a huge living room. I'm going to try and stick to that area."

"What's your plan when you get inside?"

I hadn't decided on an exact plan. I thought it over during the drive. There were a few possible scenarios. I could walk in and Keller could be alone. That would be simple. Get the confession and leave. But, if he was waiting for me, then anything could happen.

"Jack? You got a plan?"

"Winging it, big man."

Bear cursed under his breath and whipped his head side to side. "I'll go on record as saying if we die, it's on your hands."

"Sounds good."

MY BOOTS THUDDED against the white concrete sidewalk. The sound echoed through the air. I had debated whether to cut through backyards or just walk up to the house and knock. I decided to walk up to the house. I didn't care if he saw me coming. If things went the way I hoped, then he wouldn't think I was there to take him down. He would think I was there for help. On the other hand, if he knew we were coming, then he'd be prepared no matter how I entered the house.

Light shone through downstairs windows. A little white sign attached to a stake was planted at the corner of his yard. It read, "Don't walk on the lawn." I kicked the sign out of the ground and crossed the grass to the steps leading up to the front porch. I stopped in front of the red painted front door. I leaned toward the door, my head turned sideways. Silence.

The handle turned. The sound of metal clicking broke the silence. I took a step back and the door swung open. I recognized the swollen face that stared back at me. The short dark stubble on the top of his head wasn't there a couple days ago when I broke his jaw, though.

"Jarhead," he said through teeth that were wired shut. His nostrils flared and his eyes narrowed. He brought his arms in front of him and clenched his fists.

Keller stepped into view. "Hello, Jack." He stepped into the foyer and placed a hand on the young man's shoulder. "You've met my stepson, Mike."

I nodded and scanned the room behind them. Three brown leather couches formed a U shape in the middle of the room. Two small square tables joined the middle couch with the others. A plain rug covered the hardwood floor in the empty space between the couches.

"Why don't you come on in, Jack?"

Keller pulled Mike back and gestured me through the door.

I stepped in and felt his hand on my back.

"Can I take your jacket?"

I dipped my shoulder and spun around.

"No thanks."

He lifted his hands in an off-putting gesture. "No problem." He shut the front door and walked past me and took a seat on the couch facing me. "Have a seat."

"I'm fine standing."

He sighed. "What can I do for you, Jack?"

Mike walked past Keller and headed for the hall.

"I want him to stay in here," I said.

Mike kept walking.

"Mike," Keller said sternly.

The young man stopped and turned, then took a seat on the same couch as Keller.

A smug look crossed Keller's face. "Why are you here?"

"You know why."

"I'm afraid I don't."

"Four Marines are dead. Six are in prison in Iraq. Two are on the run and wanted for murders they didn't commit."

Keller shook his head.

"I don't know. There's some damning evidence against those two Marines on the run. I've seen it with my own eyes, Jack."

I said nothing.

"If you need me to help you, I might be able to arrange something. But, to be honest, killing that man in D.C., and then Abbot. Christ." He turned his head toward Mike. "Look at what you did to my boy here. The assault charge alone carries twenty years in prison."

Mike lifted his head from his chest and stared at me. His lip curled. Even in his current state I didn't doubt that he'd attack like a junkyard dog if given the command.

"I know what you did, Keller."

Keller put his hands in his pockets and cocked his head to the side. He grinned and lifted his eyebrows a half inch.

"What I did? I don't follow, Jack. What do you know?"

I took a deep breath. I had to keep my composure, for now.

"You set all of this up. You had the Iraqi family killed and then framed me for the murder." I left Bear's name out on purpose. "You didn't count on Abbot getting us home, back to the U.S., though. Did you?"

Keller sat back in the corner of the couch, crossed his arms and legs and smiled at me.

"Abbot pulled a few strings and got his guys out of there, got us out of there. He didn't know that the others had been set up yet. You had a twenty-four hour plan and set it in motion with me. You got wind of what Abbot had done and then had the plans changed. That's why the CIA met us at the airport and not Abbot or an MP."

Keller said nothing. He sat there with the same smile on his face with his eyes crinkled upward. He nodded his head slowly.

"So they took us to Camp Lejeune. Nothing out of the ordinary there, right? I had to report there at the base quarterly, at a minimum. Throwing us in the brig was a nice touch though." I waited for him to respond. He didn't. I continued. "Then you tried to have me killed, first with the psycho in the cell, which was a pathetic attempt, and then in the bathroom. Just nod if I'm right."

He sat motionless. The smile slowly faded from his face.

"Didn't count on Abbot getting McDuffie to get me out of there though, did you?"

"No, I didn't." He frowned and looked down at the floor. Back up at me.

I smiled. "You must have crapped a brick when you found out I was heading up to see Delaney. I just want to know, why didn't you have him killed before he met with me?"

"Because I wanted both of you dead and making the hit at the same time seemed the best option." He glared at me now.

"Who did Delaney work for?"

He shrugged and held out his hands. "We'll never know, will we?"

"Then you tracked me to—"

"Let me save you some time, Noble. We tracked you through your damn cell phone." He leaned forward and then stood. Crossed in front of one of the couches and then behind it, using the couch to separate us. He stopped and placed his hands on the back of the couch and hunched over it. "Tracked you to the girl's house. Thought it would be good to give you a scare before taking you out. You know, the phone call."

"All you did was gave me a head's up."

"Yeah, well..." He lifted a hand and ran it over his head. "We had the men in place to take you out."

"I saw them."

"Martinez called them back. He wanted to—"

"Martinez," I said flatly.

Keller raised his voice. "Yeah, Martinez." Then he continued. "He was about to take Abbot out. We knew you'd be heading there next, so why not try to coincide your visit with Abbot's murder, then get you at the next stop."

"Only you lost me. Isn't that right?"

"Yeah." Keller turned to glance over his shoulder, and then looked back at me. "Found your phone, though. Want it back?"

"Keep it. Hate the damn thing, anyway." I didn't give him a chance to talk. "So you gave the order to take out Abbot. Why?"

"He was going to screw it all up, Jack. Everything we had going for us."

"You hated the idea. Don't you remember that? You were pissed when you sent us off to Langley for this program."

He nodded. "After a while they, uh, helped me see the light."

"They paid you off."

He hiked his shoulders a few inches and held out his hands.

"Admit it. You were getting paid off. That's how you were able to afford this place."

"No, actually, that's not true. Nancy did get that book deal everyone talked about. We settled for this place only because I'm stuck here for a few more years."

"So what did you do with the money?"

"That's for me to worry about, Jack. And it goes beyond the money."

I studied him for a moment before responding.

"Then what?"

"Politics, Jack." He smiled and stood up straight. "The things I was doing were helping me get in with the right people."

"You murdered Abbot and a man you didn't know just so you could get a pass in D.C.?"

He smiled and winked.

I shook my head and turned toward the door.

"You might not want to leave just yet, Jack."

Mike walked past me and stood in front of the door, blocking my exit.

I laughed and looked over my shoulder at Keller. "You think he's going to stop me?"

"No," Keller said. "No, I don't. But you might want to wait a minute."

I heard footsteps echo through the room. They came from the hallway behind Keller. A man stepped out.

"Hello, Jack."

I nodded. "Martinez."

A second man appeared from the hallway. I recognized his face from the base in Iraq, but didn't know his name. His extended arm pulled at something from the hall.

Jessie.

Her glossy eyes and the tear tracks on her cheeks told me all I needed to know.

My eyes shifted from Jessie, to Keller and back to Martinez, who now aimed his pistol at me.

Keller laughed. "Didn't you think I was a bit too forthcoming with my confession, Jack?"

I felt Mike's hands touch my shoulders and then proceed to pat down my sides and my legs. He reached around my stomach. My Beretta pushed into my ribs when his hands discovered it.

"He's armed," Mike said.

Keller nodded. "Would have been surprised if he wasn't, though. Nice and slow, Jack. Put it on the floor."

I took a deep breath. I didn't know if Mike was armed or not. Martinez was and he aimed his gun at me. His partner probably was, but his weapon wasn't drawn. Keller didn't appear to be, but most likely had a weapon hidden somewhere in the room. The moment I pulled my weapon, Martinez would be on high alert and would shoot me if I made any movements that didn't lead to me putting my gun on the ground. I could try and take him out first. Two problems with that, though. One, he'd get his shot off at the same time, if not sooner. Two, his partner had Jessie and might kill her before I could manage a shot in his direction.

The next option was to take out the partner. There was nothing to stop a clean shot. Martinez would have the same clean shot on me, though. And then after he had killed me, he would kill Jessie.

"Jack," Keller said. "Remove the gun and place it on the floor. This is the last time I'll ask."

I held my hands out in front of me and then reached into my jacket. I froze in position. I had to stall as long as possible.

"Now," Keller said.

"I'm just moving nice and slow, just like you asked."

I pulled the gun from my jacket and held it out, extending my fingers so they weren't near the trigger. Martinez watched every move. He tensed. I sensed his urge to pull the trigger. He had probably dreamed of it since that night in Iraq, hell, maybe even before then. I held one arm out and gestured with the other for everyone to remain calm.

"Nice and easy," I said.

The door behind me crashed open. I didn't have to turn my head to know that Bear had kicked it in. The crash was enough to distract Martinez. I fired a shot at him. He collapsed where he stood. His partner took aim at me and I dove behind the couch and crawled toward the end. Bullets tore through the leather and thudded into the wall behind me.

Jessie's screams were silenced with a thud. I peeked over the couch and saw the man hovering over her. Then I checked over my shoulder and saw that Mike had charged Bear. The big man seemed to be handling him on his own. Keller had run upstairs. I'd deal with him in a minute.

I leapt up and fired at the man standing over Jessie. My shots missed. He dove into the hall. His footsteps echoed through the room as he ran down it. I hurried to where Jessie lay on the floor and pulled her by her feet so she was no longer an easy target. She had been knocked unconscious by the man. I moved her further away from the hall and then backed up to the wall. I peeked around the corner and was met with a hail of gunfire.

"Christ," I said. "Bear, finish him and get Jessie out of here."

The big man delivered a heavy blow to Mike's head and dropped him on the floor. He ran toward me. Dove over the couch as a shotgun blast ripped through the air from above.

"Guess Keller's weapon wasn't as close by as I thought," I said.

Bear said nothing.

I pointed toward a hall that led to the kitchen. "There's a door leading out back through there."

He nodded, scooped up Jessie and started toward the hall.

I peeked around the corner again. Empty. I moved slowly down the hall.

Each side had two doors. Three of the doors were closed. The last one on the right was open. I stopped a few feet from the door and listened. Complete silence. I checked over my shoulder to make sure Keller wasn't standing behind me. He wasn't.

I grabbed the TracFone from inside my jacket and threw it into the room. The man bumped the door as he turned to see what I threw. I exploded around the corner. He stood closer than I anticipated, and I had to strike him. I moved in sideways and hooked his right arm with my left. I applied pressure and bent his elbow in the wrong direction. He let out a roar and dropped his gun to the floor. I brought my right arm up to smack him across the face with my gun, but he managed to get his arm in between and the sudden jarring stop caused me to drop my gun too.

He continued bringing his arm forward and wrapped it around my head and took out my leg with a quick kick. A moment later he had positioned himself behind me and had me in a chokehold.

I fought for position. I fought to loosen his grip. I was losing on both counts.

"General," he yelled.

I heard Keller's footsteps as he walked down the hall. The barrel of his rifle appeared in the doorway. I knew he wouldn't be far behind.

I reached behind me and found the man's head. I jammed my thumb in his eye. That was enough to loosen his grip. I shifted my body weight and broke free from his grasp. Then I ducked and slipped behind him. I held his arm behind his back and pushed him toward the doorway.

Keller spun around and fired blindly. The bullet hit the man in the front of his chest and tore through the back, leaving an opening the size of a melon.

I lunged forward, using the wounded man as a body shield. We crashed into Keller and he fell backwards. He landed against the door across the hall. It broke from the latch and he continued his fall to the floor. He dropped the rifle. I tossed my human shield to the side and grabbed the rifle off of the floor and lifted it and aimed it at Keller.

"Jack," he said as he wiped blood from his mouth. "You don't have to do this."

"Do what?"

I fired into the back of the room.

He covered his head and cowered close to the floor.

I aimed the rifle at his head. "Get up."

He did.

"Down the hall." I backed up and let him slip by me. "Nice and easy, Keller. Arms up, hands behind your head."

He complied and walked slowly down the hall, stopping when he reached the end.

"Keep going," I said.

He took a few more steps and stopped again. I stuck the end of the rifle into his back and pushed. He took a few more steps forward. Mike was sitting on one of the couches, holding his arm to his chest. The arm was bent at an odd angle halfway between his wrist and his elbow. It had been a rough week for Mike.

"Go sit next to your son," I said.

Keller did as he was told and walked to the couch. He stopped and turned toward me.

I kept the rifle steady and aimed at his chest.

"You won't get away with this, Noble."

"Why's that?"

"You broke into my house. Attacked me and my son. Christ, look at his arm." He swung his arm to the side dramatically and pointed at his son's twisted arm. "Then you killed my guests, two government employees, Jack. You killed them in cold blood."

"Who's going to believe that story?"

He laughed. "Who wouldn't? A General versus the word of a Sergeant?" He stepped toward me. "Put the gun down, Jack. You won't get away with this. Even if you kill me, you won't get away with it."

I circled around the front of the couches, toward the front door. Kept the gun aimed at Keller.

Keller continued. "They will hunt you down, Jack. The Marines, CIA, local authorities. Hell, even the FBI will get in on the action. Everyone will want a piece of you."

"Yeah, to take the fall for the murders you committed."

"In a roundabout way, yeah, Jack. The murders are all on me. I ordered them all. But it was for a reason, Jack. A damn good reason. We have to take this fight to them, Jack. Don't you see?"

He stood ten feet from me. His head cocked to the side. The smile had left his face. He held his arms outstretched to the side.

I shifted the gun to one arm and reached inside my jacket. "Only problem, Keller," I pulled my hand out and showed him the digital recorder that had been running the entire time, "is that I got you admitting it on tape."

I stopped the recorder, hit rewind for a second and then hit play. *"The murders are all on me."* I clicked the stop button.

"Without a doubt, one hundred percent your voice, sir."

His face went pale and he backed into the wall. He shook his head and muttered something indecipherable under his breath.

I pulled the magazine from the rifle and dropped the gun on the floor. Looked around the room and soaked in the carnage. I turned and opened the door. Bear and Jessie had pulled the car to the curb and were waiting for me. I cut across the yard and got in the front seat. Bear pulled away without saying a word.

20

WE DROVE NORTH ON I-95. WASHINGTON, D.C. WAS OUR DESTINATION. I'D
wait for Marlowe by his house. Turn over the evidence and find out what
he had planned for Keller. We stopped and picked up the cheapest laptop
we could find. Jessie transferred the audio file to the computer and burned
it onto a CD.

It turned out to be a good thing she had been held hostage by Martinez,
notwithstanding the emotional scarring and baggage the ordeal would
leave her with. She kept her spirits up, though, and regularly made jokes at
my expense from the back seat.

We crossed the state line into Virginia. The topic of what her next steps
were hadn't been discussed yet. I turned in the passenger seat and looked
back at her.

"Do you want to go back home, Jess?"

"Do you think it's safe now?"

I shook my head. "Probably not."

"Yeah, I didn't think so."

"I can take you with me to New—"

"Dulles, Jack." She looked out the window to her side. "Take me to
Dulles when we get to D.C."

"Where do you plan to go?"

"I don't know." She shook her head slightly. "I don't know."

I cleared my throat and turned back to the front and stared out the window for a moment.

"What about you, Bear?"

"What do you mean?"

"Pretty sure with everything that's happened we can convince Marlowe to give you an honorable discharge."

He shrugged and didn't say anything.

I waited a moment and then continued. "You're thinking about staying in?" The thought hadn't occurred to me. I figured he was as antsy to get out as I was.

"What else am I going to do, Jack?" He placed both his hands on the steering wheel. Gripped it so tight his knuckles turned white. "I've got two years left. I'm going to finish out those two years."

Bear had principles, and the commitment he made meant a lot to him. I knew that. But what about the commitment they made to us and the fact that they broke that commitment? I don't recall reading anything on my contract that stated permission to terminate at will. I brushed the thought aside.

"You know, even if they don't scrap the program, there's no way you're going back to it."

He shrugged and looked at me for a second, then back toward the road. He quickly scanned the cars. "That's fine with me. I'll take a desk job for a couple years."

I laughed. Bear behind a desk? The big man would go crazy.

"Where the hell are they going to find a chair and desk big enough for you?"

A few seconds passed and then Bear broke out into laughter.

"I know, right. What the hell am I thinking?"

"Why don't you leave? We'll go into business together."

"Doing what? Crime scene creation?"

Doing what?

The words hung in the air above me. I hadn't given any thought to it. I had a few hopes. I hoped that Jessie would be part of my own "doing what." I hoped that I could travel for a couple months before my official retirement while using up my accrued leave pay. I hoped that something would just turn up. I'd only known the Marines, and more specifically, the joint program with the CIA. The actual Marines were a mystery to me. Before that, my future had been planned by my father and high school football coach. I tried not to think about either of them, nor the future I had left behind.

"What about you, Jack?" Bear said, interrupting my thoughts.

"I've got three months leave built up."

"So you're done?"

"Yeah, Bear," I said. "I'm done. This is it. I'm giving this tape to Marlowe and getting him to put my honorable discharge in writing, effective the last day of my leave. Then I'm going to do—" I leaned back and stared at the ceiling. "Then I don't know what I'm going to do. I'll figure it out at some point in the next three months."

He opened his mouth to say something and must have thought better of it. His grip had loosened on the steering wheel. A smile crept up on his face. He seemed relaxed. At peace. I hadn't even thought about the possibility that our partnership stressed him out.

"Bear, does being around—" I stopped mid-sentence, deciding not to go down that road. "Never mind."

"Never minded."

WE DROVE straight into the city. Bear dropped me off a couple blocks from Marlowe's place. He wanted to wait with me. I insisted that he take Jessie and find somewhere else to be in case something happened. I still didn't know if I could trust Marlowe. Sure, he gave up Keller, but he might have done it to protect himself. The fact that I returned might spur him into additional action. He might decide to get rid of me. I had no doubt that he had that power. If that happened, I didn't want Bear and Jessie in the middle. Plus, they had the backup files on the computer and the audio CD that implicated Keller behind everything.

Keller's confession was one reason I trusted Marlowe. Keller didn't mention him. Maybe he did it on purpose, though, in the event that I walked out of his house alive.

For a moment I doubted my decision to just leave Keller's house. My rational side told me he knew he was beaten. Despite his recent horrible decision-making, he had once been an honorable man. I'd only known him for eight years. He had been a good man most of those years. Those who knew him longer than that held him in high esteem. Maybe I was reaching. Maybe I was letting the fact that he had known and served with my father influence me.

I crossed the street and stood in front of Marlowe's house. I walked up the six steps to his front porch and rang the doorbell. Nobody answered. I took a seat on the third step and enjoyed the warm breeze.

The upscale neighborhood was quiet. That made it easy to hear Marlowe and his assigned agents approaching before they realized I was there. I thought about hiding on the other side of the stairwell. Instead, I sat still and kept my hands in plain view.

The agent who stared me down outside the pizzeria my first day in D.C. was the first to notice me. He drew his gun and barked orders at me. I looked past him. The second agent stood in front of Marlowe. Marlowe peered around the agent and nodded at me.

"I'm unarmed," I said. I had left my gun with Bear. Risky move, but I was over it at this point. The recording held the truth. The police could arrest me. Secret Service or the DoD could detain me. CIA and FBI could fight over who would detain me. In the end, I'd be set free by Keller's words.

"Hands up," the agent said.

"They're in plain view," I said. "Get your damn gun out of my face. OK?"

"It's OK, Gerard," Marlowe said.

The two agents relaxed a bit. Well, relaxed as much as uptight Defense Department agents could. Those guys were hardwired for action. They found it in everything they did. I bet even brushing their teeth turned into an anxiety inducing event. I wondered what the heart attack rate was for guys in their line of work within their first five years of retirement.

Marlowe pushed past the men entrusted with his life and stood on the sidewalk a few feet in front of me.

"Jack, let's go inside and talk."

I looked between him and the two men in dark suits behind him. "They have to come in with us?"

"Yes, unfortunately they have to go with me everywhere during working hours." He climbed a single step. "But they'll be well behaved. Won't you boys?" He turned and smiled at the men.

They didn't smile back.

I stood and followed Marlowe inside. It was nice going in through the front door. He led the way to the kitchen where he started a pot of coffee and pulled two beers from the refrigerator. The Defense Department agents tried to follow us in. Marlowe sent one outside through the back door, and made the other wait in the living room, telling him to stay at least ten feet from the swinging door.

He cracked open a beer and handed it to me. I took it and put it to my lips without checking the label. A few sips later I was exhaling with contentment at the refreshing beverage.

He smiled, his eyebrows rising into his forehead as he started to pour his beer into a tall glass, but then thought better of it. He pushed the glass aside and held up the bottle as though he was inspecting it.

"It's local, a craft beer. Excellent stuff. Brewer is a friend of mine."

I nodded and took another pull from the brown bottle. Still hadn't checked the label.

"Anyway, Mr. Noble," he said, "I'm sure you didn't come here to discuss local breweries."

I shook my head and didn't correct him for calling me Mister instead of Sergeant.

"I take it you confronted Keller?"

"I did."

"How did it go?"

I reached into my inside pocket and noticed Marlowe tense for a second, the smile fading from his face.

"Relax," I said as I pulled the small digital recorder from my pocket. "It's all on here."

He smiled and walked in front of me and took a seat at the table. He crossed his legs and took a long pull on his beer, then set the bottle down on the table.

"Play it."

I hit play and placed the digital recorder on the table. Marlowe listened intently, nodding and making eye contact with me occasionally.

"That's some pretty damning evidence," he said.

"I've got copies."

He smiled and reached for the recorder. "Don't worry, Jack. I'll handle this."

I grabbed the recorder and pulled it closer. "What will happen to Keller?"

He took another pull from his bottle of beer and stared at me for a moment. "Worst case is a dishonorable discharge."

"No jail time?"

"I hope so, but you know there are many parties involved in this. It's up to them how they want to pursue the matter. Implicating Keller might implicate them."

I shook my head. "He's responsible for the deaths of at least ten people."

"I know that and you know that. Hell, the person responsible for making this decision will know it." He got up and went to the fridge and came back with two more beers, already opened. "This is the dark side of these operations, Jack."

I nodded. I knew. I knew when I was in his house that it might end up like this. I wanted to kick myself for not taking him out when I had the chance.

"What about me?" I said.

"What about you?" he said.

"I want out."

"Jack, I'm pretty sure that even if the program is continued, you won't be invited back in."

"Not just the program. I want out of the Marines. My enlistment is up in September. I've got three months leave accrued. I'm taking my leave and I want my official retirement to be the last day of my leave."

"I don't have the power to—"

"Bullshit, Marlowe."

He shifted in his seat. Crossed his arms over his chest and looked me over.

"Ok, Jack."

He pulled a cell phone from his coat and placed a call. Five minutes later I had my freedom. He also instructed whoever he spoke with to remove me and Bear from any federal, state and local suspect lists.

"You're free, Mr. Noble."

I slid the digital recorder across the table. Marlowe picked it up, studied it and then dropped it into his glass of beer.

"Why?" I tried to appear angry, but felt confused. He knew I had a backup. Did he expect me to push this further or in a different direction? Was this his way of telling me he wasn't going to do anything?

"Political suicide, Jack. On top of that, imagine when the media gets a hold of this information. A Marine General ordering the deaths of his own men and another commanding officer? It's best to leave it be, Jack. I'll take care of Keller in my own way."

So that was it. He was going to take the political route. He could squeeze anyone I presented the evidence to. I felt like reaching out and striking him. I didn't. I'd still present the CD to a few contacts and see where we could take it.

I nodded and stood and grabbed the bottle of beer off the table and finished it one pull. I spun the bottle in my hand and the label caught my eye, a coat of arms with two broadswords crossing one another. *Double Crossed Breweries.* Perfect.

"You did the right thing, Jack. No matter what happens to Keller. Who knows how many lives you saved?"

"Not enough," I said. "One question, though. If you knew, why didn't you come down on Keller?"

"I didn't know. Not one hundred percent. It made sense. Evidence pointed that way. But I would have never got the confession that you did."

"Not that the confession matters." I turned and pushed through the door without saying another word.

TWO HOURS later I stood outside Dulles airport with Bear and Jessie. Bear leaned against a glass wall ten yards away while I talked to Jessie. The sound of planes taking off and landing roared through the air with a rhythmic beat.

"Don't go, Jess."

She smiled and leaned forward. "It won't work, Jack, at least not now."

"Why?"

"You need time. I need time. We both need—"

"Time," I said. "Yeah, I got it."

I turned my head and tried to think of something to say, anything to stop her from leaving.

"What about the other night? I thought that we made, you know, a connection."

"I think that was just the surprise of seeing you after so long. It's true I haven't stopped loving you, Jack. But that doesn't mean we're meant to be together."

"I'm taking three months and getting away. Doing some traveling. I'm going to get my head straight. Back to who I was."

"You are who you were. And you can't change who you are now."

She glanced at her watch.

"Let's give it a month or so, then. What do you say, Jess?"

She placed a finger to my mouth. Leaned forward and kissed me.

"I have to go now."

She placed a folded piece of paper in my hand. "That's my email address." She turned and walked through the door, into the main terminal.

Bear pushed off the wall and walked toward me, his hand extended. I grabbed it and shook.

"Don't know what I'm going to do without you around, brother."

He smiled and wrapped his arm around me. We patted at each other's backs for a few seconds and then took a step back. He reached down and picked up his bag and gave me a wink. We didn't say another word. He turned and disappeared through the same set of doors as Jessie.

I stood in the middle of the walkway for five minutes, nearly every fiber of my being told me to follow her. I didn't, though. Instead, I returned to the rental car and left the airport. Inside the car, I popped the CD that had the recording of Keller's confession into the car's CD player. All that came through the speakers was silence. The CD was blank. It contained no confession and no evidence. Jessie had the laptop that held the original file. I had a feeling the track was gone. I cursed under my breath and slammed my fists into the dashboard. I pulled the car over onto the emergency shoulder and tried to call Bear. No answer. He had already turned his phone off. I thought about who else to call, but came up with no names. I had nowhere to go. In the end I decided to let it go. It didn't matter. I'd check in on Keller's status, and if I wasn't satisfied, I'd take care of it myself one day.

I found my way to the interstate and headed north for New York City. Bear hit up a few of his contacts and found Abbot's daughter using the number I swiped from his phone. I promised him I'd look out for her, and I'd start by letting her know her father had passed. According to Bear's contact, no next of kin had been informed yet.

It took just under three hours to make it to the city. I found a parking garage within a few miles of her apartment and ditched the car. She had a place in the Village on Bedford Street. I walked from the parking lot to her apartment building. The air was cooler here than in D.C. Still, not too bad for six in the evening. The sun was setting and streetlights were kicking on. I passed a coffee shop and stopped in for a cup, partly because I needed the burst of caffeine, and partly because I dreaded giving Clarissa the news.

I took my time drinking the coffee and reading a few pages of the newspaper that had been left on the table. It revealed that there was nothing new in the world. It had been six months since the attacks on the Twin Towers. I wondered if life was truly back to normal here in the city. I knew it wasn't for me. I wondered if it ever would be.

I assumed the teams were still operating in Afghanistan. I hoped that the combined power of the CIA and Armed Forces Spec Ops teams would bring Bin Laden and all those involved to justice, no matter how long it took. Our involvement in Iraq worried me. It seemed like a foregone conclusion that the work we were doing there would lead to more conflict.

The waitress interrupted my thoughts and asked if I'd like anything else. I smiled and told her no. I dropped a twenty on the table and left before she brought the check.

Clarissa's apartment was only a few blocks from the coffee shop. Despite its close proximity, it took me half an hour to reach it. I stood in front of the cracked green painted door for another five minutes before knocking.

She answered the door. Squinted at me and then smiled.

"Jack?"

It had been a few years since I had last seen her. She was still a scrawny teen at that time. She wasn't much older than a teen now, if at all, but she sure as hell wasn't scrawny anymore. The little girl I'd met all those years ago was now a woman.

"Hey, Clarissa," I said.

She reached out and hugged me.

"What are you doing here?"

"Can I come in?"

"Yeah, sure." She took a step back and pulled the door open. She waved me through and closed and locked the door behind me. "Make yourself comfortable. Can I get you a drink?"

"Nah, I mean, yeah. Something hard. Got any whiskey?"

"Sure," she said as she crossed the room to the kitchen.

"Can I smoke in here?"

"Yeah, there's an ashtray on the table in front of you."

I smiled. I hadn't noticed it. I hadn't been able to take my eyes off of her since I stepped through the door. I lit a cigarette and leaned over the coffee table. I tried a dozen times to start the inevitable conversation while she fixed my drink.

She returned to the room, set the drink in front of me and took a seat across from me.

"What brings you to New York, Jack?"

I took a drink from the glass. The hard liquor burned down my throat and warmed my stomach.

"I don't know how to put this, so I'm just going to say it."

She sat back and crossed her arms. One hand went to her chin. Her eyes grew wide and she bit her bottom lip.

"Your father is dead. He was murdered."

She gasped and took a deep breath. Her green eyes watered and a tear slipped past the corner of her bottom lid and traveled down her cheek.

"I killed the man who did it. Got a confession from the man who arranged it."

"Who? Who was it?"

"You don't know the man who pulled the trigger. Martinez, a CIA asshole. But the man..." My voice trailed off. She knew Keller. The first time I met her, Keller was there. Keller and Abbot had been close. The man was like an uncle to her. "Keller. It was General Keller who ordered it."

She lifted her eyebrows and leaned forward. The tears flowed faster.

I set my drink down and slid off the couch. I walked over to her and dropped to my knees in front of her. Wrapped my arms around her and held her tight. She cried and talked, then cried some more. I held her and listened. We stayed up late into the morning hours, drinking and smoking. By the end of the night she seemed at peace with her father's passing. Or maybe she was drunk enough that she'd gone numb.

The next morning I woke up on her couch with a slight headache. She was in the kitchen making breakfast. I walked over and sat down at the breakfast counter.

"I'm going on a trip for three months. But I've got a new cell phone and will be available if you need anything." I put my new phone up on the counter. It was a hell of a phone. It connected to the internet and could even send emails. The guy that sold it to me was completely geeked out about it. I really didn't care, but since I would be traveling, I figured it would be a good thing to have. Maybe the email part would help me to reconnect with Jessie. Although, at that moment, I was struggling to recall much about her.

Clarissa turned and smiled.

"If you want to tag along, you're welcome to do so," I said.

She laughed and walked over to the counter and leaned into it, facing me. I had to fight back the urge to kiss her.

"I haven't seen you in, what, four or five years now? And you want to walk in and sweep me off my feet?"

I smiled and looked away. "It's not that. I promised your dad I'd take care of you. Watch over you."

"Honey, I've been watching over myself for years. I'll be OK."

"Well, give me your email address so I can keep up with you."

She laughed and snatched my phone off the counter. A minute later she set it back down in front of me. "It's in there now."

Great, I thought. *Now I just need to figure out how to access it.*

A minute later she set a plate with two eggs and five strips of bacon in front of me. I ate it quickly and then got to my feet. I wrote my phone number down and left it on the middle of the counter.

"I'll be in touch," I said.

She met me at the door and gave me a hug and a kiss on the cheek. Her mouth lingered there for longer than it should have. I thought about turning my head and brushing her lips with mine. I wanted to turn my head. In the end, I didn't. It didn't feel right. Too close to her father's death.

"See ya," she said as she closed the door behind me.

21

IT TURNED OUT I DIDN'T TRAVEL ALL THAT MUCH. I TOOK A PLANE TO MIAMI, a cab across a few bridges and found a small apartment above a bar for rent in the Keys. Two and a half relaxing months passed in the blink of an eye. The place was above a locals bar. At least the majority of its patrons were locals. I made a few friends. My hair grew longer, as did my beard. It felt awkward, but I went with it.

I kept in touch with Clarissa. We talked or emailed once a week. She had moved on and seemed to be doing well for herself. Her father's life insurance policy paid nicely and would take care of her for a while. I encouraged her to use the money to go to college. She planned to spend it all on a two-year journey through Europe.

I had emailed Jessie soon after arriving here and asked her to join me. She only replied with a maybe and an apology for deleting the file and not burning it to the CD. She feared for her parents' safety. Martinez and Keller had threatened her that day they held her hostage. I was pissed that I had trusted her enough to handle the CD. Should have done it myself or at least watched over the process. I told her not to worry about it. Under the circumstances, I understood. Gave her a deadline to come to the Keys and told her that after that point I'd be unavailable. I don't know if that statement had any truth to it or not, but I couldn't go on waiting forever.

The deadline loomed, now just a few hours away.

I sat outside at a table on the bar's patio. On either side of me was an empty bistro table. A few people joined me throughout the day. They'd stay anywhere from a couple minutes up to an hour. It just depended on who and where the conversation went. I stayed sober during most of the day and only started drinking around two that afternoon. At four I didn't feel drunk, but I certainly felt the effects of the alcohol.

"Noble," a voice called through the open window just above my head.

"Yeah," I said without looking back or standing.

"Got a call for you."

I looked at my watch. Four fifteen.

"Man or woman?"

"Man."

"Take a message." I didn't feel like talking.

My spot had a nice view of the water. Not a full view, but decent enough. It was early June. The sun stayed out until close to nine at night. I had every intention of sitting there until then. I had told Jessie six p.m. But I'd wait until nine. Or until I drank enough that I couldn't sit upright anymore.

As the next two hours passed, I found myself looking further and further down the street in an effort to spot her.

"Today's the day, eh, Noble?"

I smiled at the elderly couple who sat down at the table with me. Ralph had been a computer salesman in upstate New York. He and Marcy had been married for forty years. They left the cold a few years back for the laid-back lifestyle the Keys could offer those with the money to afford it.

Marcy straightened Ralph's blue Hawaiian print button up shirt and then leaned toward me.

"She'll show, Jackie."

Most people here simply called me Noble. For some reason, Marcy saw me as the son or grandson she never had and insisted on calling me Jackie. I stopped protesting after the first week. It was quite obvious she wasn't changing her stance.

"We'll see."

"Don't get his hopes up, Marcy."

186

"Thanks for the vote of confidence, Ralph," I said.

We talked for half an hour about nothing in particular. They offered to pay for my drinks. I declined and paid for theirs. It was a game of sorts, who could throw their hands up and protest the longest and the loudest. Four times out of five, they won. Tonight they let me take the glory.

Ralph looked down at his watch. "Six p.m. We should go and leave you to your woman." He winked and helped Marcy out of her chair. The couple joined hands and slipped through the open entrance of the bar and joined the rest of the Key West crowd who had become my family.

Six o'clock passed, and there was no sign of Jessie. I leaned back in my seat and stared out at the ocean. I lost myself in the crystal blue waters and sounds of locals and tourists on the street and beach. I had dropped into such a deep zone that I didn't notice someone standing in front of me.

I shifted my gaze and looked at the person. It wasn't who I hoped it would be.

"Jack Noble." Not a question. The man knew me. He stood with his hands on his hips. His jacket pushed just enough to the side that I could see the handle of his pistol. What I didn't see was a badge. He had to be a fed, though. Who the hell would be in Key West dressed in a suit in the middle of June? I found myself wishing I still carried a gun with me everywhere I went. Unfortunately, it didn't jive with swim trunks and a tank top.

"Do I know you, friend?" I'd taken to calling strangers friend. Everyone down here was a friend. I couldn't help thinking this was the life I could have had during off seasons and after my pro football career.

"I've got a proposition for you."

"Does it involve handcuffs and a nine by nine cell? If so, I'm not interested."

He laughed and pulled out a chair. "May I?"

"Have at it."

He sat down and looked up at the open window. "Uh, sure, whatever he's having." He looked back at me and smiled.

I looked away.

"This has nothing to do with handcuffs or cells. I want to offer you a job."

"Doing what?"

"Well, that's complicated. You see—"

"Let me save you the time. No." I grabbed my glass and took a sip. "I'm not interested in working."

"You've got two weeks left until your government hand out ends."

"Hey," I said as I pointed at him. "I worked hard for that money. Went three years without a vacation. Don't go around telling me it's a freebie. And keep your damn voice down."

"Apologies, on all counts." He stood and took his drink from the bartender's outstretched hand. "Ten years or so with us and you'll never have to worry about money again."

"Who are you?"

"Name's Frank."

I waited for him to tell me his last name. He didn't.

"Who do you work for?"

"That's classified."

"Not the FBI. No badge."

He nodded

"CIA wouldn't want anything to do with me."

"Correct again."

"NSA?"

He shook his head.

"Then who—"

"I'll save you some time, Noble. The only way you'll find out is if you join."

I looked around the street and didn't notice anyone.

"What's the job description?"

"Professional killer."

I lifted an eyebrow. He smiled. It wasn't the smile of someone that just told a joke. He meant business. It made sense. All my training had led to this.

"Who told you about me?"

"I, uh, I really can't tell you that."

"Marlowe."

He shrugged.

It was Marlowe.

"I need a bit to decide."

"You've got two minutes, Jack. After that, I leave."

My mind started on the *what if* game. What if Jessie showed up? What if she didn't? I was terrified of both. But the thing that kept pushing its way to the front of my mind was that I wanted to join Frank and his mystery organization. I wanted to be a part of the team. I craned my neck and looked down both sides of the street. I didn't see her. I knew I wouldn't see her. Not here. Not anywhere, never again.

"I'm in," I said.

Frank stood and extended his hand. I reached up and shook it. He smiled at me for a moment and pulled a card from his pocket. He let go of my hand and pulled a pen from inside his jacket and wrote something down on the card.

"Two weeks," he said and then he turned and left.

I placed the card on the table, then finished my drink while keeping my eyes open and aware. I kept up hope that Jessie would show up. She didn't. At nine p.m., after a glorious sunset full of deep reds, oranges and pinks, I stood and grabbed the card off the table. It took a few minutes for my drunken eyes to focus. I read the note out loud.

"July 1st. East 64th Street and Park Avenue. Ten in the morning." Below that line it said, "Welcome aboard, Noble."

THE END

The story continues in A Deadly Distance, Jack Noble #2. Continue to read an excerpt.

Sign up for L.T. Ryan's new release newsletter and be the first to find out when new Jack Noble novels are published. To sign up, simply fill out the form on the following page:

https://ltryan.com/newsletter/

As a thank you for signing up, you'll receive a complimentary digital copy of *The First Deception (Jack Noble Prequel)* with bonus story *The Recruit: A Jack Noble Short Story.*

If you enjoyed reading *Noble Beginnings: A Jack Noble Thriller*, I would appreciate it if you would help others enjoy this book, too. How?

Lend it. This e-book is lending-enabled, so please, feel free to share it with a friend. All they need is an amazon account and a Kindle, or Kindle reading app on their smart phone or computer.

Recommend it. Please help other readers find this book by recommending it to friends, readers' groups and discussion boards.

Review it. Please tell other readers why you liked this book by reviewing it at Amazon, Barnes & Noble, Apple or Goodreads. Your opinion goes a long way in helping others decide if a book is for them. Also, a review doesn't have to be a big old book report. If you do write a review, please send me an email at contact@ltryan.com so I can thank you with a personal email.

Like Jack. Visit the Jack Noble Facebook page and give it a like: https://www.facebook.com/JackNobleBooks.

And then join us in my private Facebook group: https://www.facebook.com/groups/1727449564174357.

A DEADLY DISTANCE: CHAPTER 1

Six feet. A deadly distance. Especially when one man has a gun aimed at another. Close enough to take missing out of the equation. Far enough away that the target has slightly more than a zero percent chance of making a move, whether to disarm the assailant or duck and cover.

The guy I'd been hunting in the dusty and dimly lit warehouse found me first. I had taken a set of splintered wooden stairs to the catwalk that wrapped the interior edges of the building and cut across the center of the large rectangular room. I hustled up the steps, two at a time. The old wooden boards sagged and creaked and moaned, but held under my weight. The catwalk was stronger, sturdier. It didn't move in response to me. No bouncing. No side-to-side sway. One foot fell in front of the other as I side-stepped along the catwalk. I let my feet hit the floor from the outside in, minimizing the noise. Still, the planks gave off a slight thump in response to my boots hitting the wood. I knew if I wasn't careful, he'd hear me.

And he did.

Fortunately, I heard his footsteps, too. Unfortunately, I only heard them a second before he spoke.

"Stop," he said. His accent was thick. South American. "Drop your gun."

I froze and lifted my hands. The gun swung like a pendulum, upside down and with only my index finger holding it up by the trigger guard.

"Drop it," he said.

I dipped my finger to the side and let the gun slide off and over the railing. It hit the floor with a thud, managing to not discharge a round. The cold handle of my backup piece rested reassuringly against my lower back, sending chills through me as the cold metal touched my sweaty skin.

"Now turn around," he said.

I turned in a half-circle and got my first good look at the man I'd been chasing for the last twenty minutes. He stood approximately five foot nine. Weighed probably one-eighty. He wore a tan jacket and black knit cap. Sparse dark hair covered his cheeks and chin. His eyes matched his hair. He stood six feet away, a pistol held close to his chest and aimed at me. A distance of six feet increased his odds of being deadly accurate. A distance of six feet reduced my chances of effectively neutralizing him. Even at six-two, my reach wasn't enough to land a blow.

"Who the hell are you?" he said.

"I'm the man who was sent to kill you," I said.

"By who?"

"What?"

"Who's your boss?"

"Why?"

"Because I want to write him a letter to recommend he fire you."

I chuckled. The guy had a sense of humor, only the look on his face said he wasn't joking.

"Why's that?" I said.

"Because you failed this class, asshole." He lifted the barrel of the gun and waved it back and forth, like a mother scolding her toddler.

"Only problem," I said, "is this is only recess. Playtime for you."

The man forced a laugh. "You're the one following me, so you must have some idea who I am."

"Not really." And that was the truth. Frank Skinner and I had acted on a single piece of information that said a man fitting the guy's description would be waiting at a bus stop.

"Well let me give you the abridged version," he said. "I'm someone you shouldn't be following. You should have done your homework first. Now it's too late for you."

I smiled. "First, enough with the school analogies. Second, it's never too late for me."

His eyes narrowed. He brought his left hand up and wiped his cheek with his palm. His eyes darted upward and mine followed along. Light shone through a tiny hole in the roof. Bright, but gray. Rain water dripped through the hole and spattered the man's face. He cursed under his breath. He'd have to move and his next step would seal my fate.

The man didn't move, though. Not immediately, at least. Two more drops hit him. Then a third. Finally, he cursed and took a step forward. Six feet had been reduced to five. Still out of my reach, but not by much. If I lunged forward, I could reach him in one step instead of two.

"Just give it up," I said. "We've got the warehouse surrounded. You won't make it out of here."

"Then neither will you." His eyes widened and he stuck his arm all the way out. Another mistake. His wrist flicked up and down, jerking the gun in and out of aim.

I saw my opportunity. The distance between me and the gun had been reduced by at least two-and-a-half feet. A full step and I'd have him by the wrist, neutralizing the immediate threat.

A crashing sound to my right startled both of us. I turned my head and saw a door to the outside open. Light flooded the ground floor of the warehouse. The silhouette of a man slipped through the opening and then disappeared into the shadows. I had lied when I said we had the building surrounded. There were only two of us, and I had left Frank behind a block away from the building. Either he had caught up, or the man hadn't been alone, in which case it would be two against me.

"Freeze!" Frank's voice echoed through the warehouse.

The man forgot about me and turned toward Frank. Bright muzzle blast exploded in front of me as he opened fire on Frank.

Frank didn't return fire, hopefully in an effort to not wound me, and not because he'd been hit. I couldn't worry about that, though. The man stood five feet away, his body turned and his arms outstretched over the steel railing.

I lunged forward, left arm out, right arm up. I closed the distance before the man could react. I wrapped my left hand around his throat from the side, letting my thumb slide just below his Adam's Apple. He grunted against the pressure. At the same time I drove my right arm down, catching him on his wrist, which extended out a few feet over the railing. I twisted his arm and drove it down into the steel railing. Bone and steel met with a sickening crack. He screamed. His broken arm could no longer muster up the strength required to hold the sidearm, and he dropped it. It hit the floor below us with a clank.

"Frank?" I yelled.

No answer.

The man reached across his body with his left arm and punched at my face, his fist connecting with my nose. Although he didn't have enough momentum to do any real damage, the blow managed to disrupt my grip on his neck. My eyes flooded with tears. I felt him break away from my grasp.

"My arm," he said. "You bastard, you broke my damn arm."

I heard the sound of a knife being pulled from a sheath. Blade against leather. I brought my palms to my eyes and wiped away the tears that blurred my vision. Once again, the man stood six feet away from me. His right arm pressed against his chest. In his left, he held a knife with a six inch blade. The light caught the stainless steel blade as he twirled it in his palm.

This time six feet didn't matter. I didn't have to contend with a bullet. In a fluid motion, I lunged forward and grabbed the railing on either side with both hands. Then I swung my legs forward while drawing my knees in. I drove the soles of my combat boots into his chest. He shrieked as they connected with his broken arm. The knife fell from his hand and bounced off the catwalk and fell to the concrete warehouse floor.

My momentum carried my body through, knocking the man down. He turned onto his stomach and began crawling away. His left arm scraped and scratched against the worn wooden planks.

"Jack," Frank shouted from below.

I said nothing. Walked up behind the man. Stood over him. I reached down and wrapped my right arm around his neck. His pulse thumped hard against the crook of my arm. I reached around with my left arm and grabbed my right elbow and pulled back hard. The movement squeezed the man's neck shut. I didn't care whether he died from asphyxiation, a broken neck, or if his head popped off.

The man clawed at my forearm. He swung his hips side to side, but he was no match for me. Desperate attempts to breathe were cut off by the force I exerted against his trachea.

"Jack, let him go."

I looked up and saw Frank standing at the end of the catwalk.

"Come on, Jack," he said. "We need this guy. He's got info for us."

"I don't care," I said as I squeezed tighter.

Frank approached with a hint of caution, perhaps thinking I'd snapped. He'd have been right if he thought it, too. "Let him go, Jack. Let's get him to the office and question him. Then you can do whatever you want to him."

The man's knit cap had fallen off and his sweat soaked hair brushed against my face as his body went limp. I pulled back. Looked at Frank and then the man. Frank's words filtered through the rage that kept me from thinking straight, and suddenly they made sense. I let go of the man. His body fell against the catwalk, limp and lifeless.

I reached over and grabbed the railing and pulled myself up. "Christ, I think I killed him."

Frank tucked his gun and squatted down. He reached out and placed his hand on the man's neck. After a few seconds, he said, "He's got a pulse. Help me get him downstairs and into the car."

"So that's where you were," I said. "Pulling the car around instead of chasing him in here with me."

"You just took off, Jack. I lost you." He looked up and I met his gaze with a smile.

"Just giving you a hard time." I bent over and scooped my hands under the man's shoulders. Lifted him up. Frank grabbed his legs and we carried him down the rickety stairs, which screamed in response to close to six hundred pounds of force pressing down on them.

Frank parked the car just outside the warehouse entrance, trunk to door.

"I'm gonna make sure it's clear out there," he said.

I nodded and leaned against the heavy steel framed door for support. The man started to come to. He coughed a few times and a deep, guttural groan emanated from his throat. I thought about rendering him unconscious again, but decided against it. A blow to the head might dampen his memory, and we needed to know everything that he knew.

Frank opened the back door on the driver's side of his Lincoln and gestured for me to come out.

I backed out of the warehouse, dragging the guy with me. I looked to the left and to the right. The area was empty. I didn't bother to stare into windows, though. If someone was watching us, so be it. We'd be gone by the time the cops came. And even if they caught up to us, there was little they could do. We were, for all intents and purposes, untouchable.

The rain had stopped and the sun peeked through the melting clouds. The light penetrated my eyes like shards of glass. Cold wind whipped around the sides of the building and met where we stood. It felt like getting pelted with iced over snowballs from both sides.

"Give me a hand," I said.

Frank came closer and reached out for the man's right arm in an effort to stabilize it. Together we slid him into the backseat and buckled him in. I handcuffed his left wrist to the metal post that connected the headrest to the passenger's seat.

"Sit in back with him," Frank said. "If he gets out of line," he looked at the man and smiled, "well, you know what to do."

I nodded, then walked around the back of the car and got in on the opposite side. I slid in next to the man and, for the first time, realized that he smelled like he hadn't showered in a week.

"If you hadn't been armed, I'd have thought you were a bum," I said.

The man pursed his lips and spit. His saliva smattering the back of the seat in front of him as well as the center console next to Frank.

I drove my elbow into his solar plexus. He coughed an exhale as the air drained from his lungs. His body doubled over, chin to knees.

"Try it again," I said.

He turned his head toward me. His face was deep red and the veins in his forehead stuck out like a snake swimming through water. His mouth opened and closed like a fish out of water as he tried to suck in air, but couldn't.

"Keep him quiet," Frank said.

I nodded. Looked at the man as he held his arm close to his chest. I said to Frank, "Go ahead and call the doc in to set and splint that arm."

A DEADLY DISTANCE: CHAPTER 2

Frank drove us to SIS's unofficial headquarters. Though we said unofficial, the building outside of Washington, D.C. was our primary location. However, any building we occupied for the purpose of advancing our mission would be considered our headquarters and always labeled unofficial. The SIS was an agency that didn't exist. The primary focus of the group was counter-terrorism. We had complete and total autonomy. We could push any other agency to the back of the line if we felt our cause took precedence. The agents in our group were considered elite, and often hand-picked from among the top recruits of the CIA, FBI and DEA. Only a handful of politicians and higher ups in the military knew of the agency's existence, and if you asked them, they'd flat out deny it. Even if there was a gun to their head.

We pulled up around the rear of the building. Frank stopped in front of what appeared to be a wall. If you stood close enough, and in the right, spot you'd see a tiny crack that ran up its center, then turned to the right and met another thin crack. Frank pulled a device out of his pocket and pushed a button. A wide door opened out and Frank drove into a dark garage. The place was empty except for my car, a large SUV, and a four door maroon Lexus that belonged to the doctor.

I waited in the back seat after Frank parked and cut the engine. He got out, walked around the back and opened the door next to the man. I removed the handcuff from his left wrist and pushed the man out while Frank pulled. The guy stumbled out and fell to the ground. He groaned and clutched at his broken arm.

"Get up," Frank told the guy.

I slid through the open door. The guy was on his knees, bent over with his forehead resting on the concrete floor. I grabbed him by his shirt collar and pulled the man's upper body straight up. Frank reached under his left arm and started pulling. I grabbed his collar and the waistband of his pants. We got him to his feet, then led him to the only door in the garage.

Frank swiped an access card through a security card reader and the light changed from red to green. He then placed his thumb on a pad. There was a series of beeps, and another light turned from red to green. Then the lock clicked and Frank turned the door handle. We walked down a short hall and came to the area of the main floor that we called the lobby. There were two doors on the far wall. Each door led to an interrogation room. A four by six foot mirrored window was placed a foot away from each door. Opposite the interrogation rooms was our infirmary, a state of the art medical facility that was equipped for everything from bee stings to surgery. There were six offices in the lobby, three on the north wall, three on the south. My office was next to Frank's. The third office on our side was designated for all of team B.

The stale air of the lobby enveloped us. The smell of ammonia hardly affected me anymore, but the guy we were dragging down the hall coughed and gagged as he breathed in the fumes.

The doctor stood in the doorway of the infirmary. He was tall and middle-aged. His full head of hair was half brown, half gray. His long, pointy nose was the only distinguishing feature on his face. He nodded toward our prisoner. "What's wrong with him?"

"Broken arm," I said. "Maybe a concussion, too. But that shouldn't matter."

The doctor shrugged and nodded over his shoulder. "Drop him in there."

"You want one of us to stay?" I asked.

"Him." The doctor pointed at Frank. "You ask too many questions, Mr. Noble."

Frank laughed and the doctor joined in. I said nothing. He had a point. I did tend to ask a lot of questions when he was working on one of us. I often thought that if my life had gone a bit differently when I was young, I could have ended up a doctor or trauma surgeon.

I left the infirmary and went to my office. I stacked a few manila folders and moved them to the corner of the desk, then started a pot of coffee. The rich aroma of the dark grinds soaked the air in my office. I didn't feel like waiting for the full pot to brew, so I emptied it into a stained mug as soon as there was enough. I held the mug in both hands and leaned back in my chair. The caffeine coursed through my veins, providing the jolt I needed.

I got up and left my office and walked back to the infirmary. Frank glanced at me and said nothing. He concentrated on the guy's broken arm. I took a few more steps and stopped inside the doorway and leaned against the frame.

"Out," the doctor said.

I could tell by his tone that he was serious. We tried hard to not piss Doc off, because you never knew when you were going to need him to treat you. I shrugged and backed up a few feet. Turned around and leaned back against the wall a couple yards from the door. I lifted the coffee to my face and inhaled. Steam singed the inside of my nose, just for a second. I took a sip. It was strong. Perhaps a bit too strong, if there was such a thing. I decided it didn't matter. The brew helped clear the cobwebs from my head, and that was always welcome.

Behind me, I heard the sound of bone grating against bone. The doctor was setting the fracture. The man screamed as his ulna and then radius were placed in their natural positions. I took his cries of pain as a sign that the doctor hadn't bothered to numb the guy up. I was OK with that, and apparently Frank was too. Why waste our supplies on a criminal?

With the doctor almost finished, I started to think about what questions to ask the man. We didn't know much about him, except that he showed up at a place that our intel indicated would be a spot where something would happen. But we had no idea who this guy was. What was he doing near the bus stop? Was he a part of the group we were tracking, or just doing business with them? Why did he run from us? Why did he try to kill me?

Both Frank and I had a feeling we were closing in on something big. Every piece of evidence we had gathered so far pointed to this being a terrorist cell. The only good thing about that was that we didn't have to turn it over to the FBI or DEA. These guys had been running drugs and guns and smuggling people in and out of the States for months. If it were just one of those activities, we'd be out of the loop. But it wasn't just one activity, it was the full gamut.

It also appeared that they had funding from some big businesses in hostile places, as well as possible connections with powerful people in the U.S. Homeland tried to take over on account of this, but Frank managed to push them back.

The men themselves were a mix of U.S. citizens, Colombians, and guys from the Middle East. That was the only thing that clouded our initial assumption. Why were so many different groups working together? I hoped that this guy, who looked like he might be Colombian, could tie some of those loose ends together for us. Assuming he talked, that is.

"OK, Mr. Noble," the doctor said from the other side of the wall. "He's all yours."

I drank the last of my coffee and pushed off of the infirmary wall. Met Frank and the man at the entrance. The doctor had set the bone and placed an air cast over the man's forearm. The guy sat on the edge of the gurney, shoulders slumped, head hanging, and eyes focused on the floor.

"Take him to room one," I said to Frank. Then I turned to the doctor. "Can he hold up?"

The doctor shrugged. "Maybe. I'll stick around. I've got a few things that can help keep him up and awake through whatever you do to him."

"You won't want to watch if it gets to that."

"With what you guys pay me, I can watch anything."

"Go wait in your office. We'll get you if we need you."

The doctor held up his hands. He then crossed the room and went into his office, which was on the wall opposite of mine. He closed his door and took a seat behind his computer. I glanced in as I passed and saw the familiar green game board of computer solitaire.

Frank had placed the guy in the interrogation room and now stood on the outside, watching the man through the smoky mirrored glass.

"What do you think?" I said as I stopped next to him, a few feet separating us.

"No doubt he's got information. And if our intel was right, he was at that bus stop for a reason."

I nodded. Said nothing, waiting for Frank to continue.

"Something was about to go down," Frank said.

I nodded again. Remained quiet.

"Question is what, Jack? And is he one of them? Or was he there to meet them?"

"Great questions, Frank," I said. "Only one way to find out."

He nodded and smiled. "You ready?"

"Not quite." I took two steps to the right and adjusted the thermostat, turning it down to fifty degrees. "Let's freeze him out for a bit."

Half an hour passed while we downed two cups of coffee each and smoked a few cigarettes. Neither of us said much. After two years of working together, there was no need for idle banter between us. Both of us knew what needed to be done. We each had our own tactics, and they played well off one another.

I got up and went to check on the man. He looked considerably uncomfortable. "Let's go, Frank."

Frank entered the room ahead of me. He sat at the far end of a rectangular wooden table. I sat in the middle, opposite our prisoner. The man looked between us. His lips quivered and his teeth chattered. He sniffled and shivered.

"Can we get you anything?" Frank asked.

"A coat," the man replied.

"We can do that," Frank said. "Can't we, Jack?"

I nodded. "Sure, but first you need to answer a few questions for us."

The man stared at a spot on the table and said nothing.

"What's your name?" I said.

The man said nothing.

"Your name?" I said again.

"Pablo," he said without looking up.

"What were you doing at that bus stop?" I said.

The man slowly turned his head. His teeth stopped chattering as he clenched his jaw. Muscles rippled at the bottom corners of his face. He licked his lips and calmly said, "I want my lawyer. I'm not saying anything until my lawyer is here."

Frank laughed. "I'm sorry. Do you think you have rights down here? Jack, did you read this guy his rights?"

I shook my head. Said nothing.

Frank stood and positioned himself next to me, across the table from the guy. "OK, asshole, here are your rights. You have the right to sit in that chair. You have the right to answer every friggin' question we ask you. You don't have the right to remain silent. Your efforts to remain silent are going to be met with a pain so intense you'll wish we had amputated your arm instead of just breaking it. You don't get a lawyer or a chaplain or your mommy. That doctor over there, he's on our side. He can give you medication to keep you awake through any amount of pain we put you through. You won't pass out, asshole. You'll cry until you have no more tears. You'll puke until all your stomach is barren and all you can do is dry heave. So answer my partner's question or your pain is going to start in about thirty seconds."

The man clenched the fist of his good arm. His eyes watered. I assumed the reality of the situation hit him at that moment. We weren't the cops and there was nothing legal about us, at least not in any sense that he, or most people, understood. Frank and I were authorized to do our jobs, no matter what it took. We could come and go and shoot to kill without asking questions, and without having questions asked of us.

Frank placed both hands on the table and leaned over until he was no more than a foot from the guy's face. "So what's it gonna be?"

The man pulled his head back a few inches. His lips thinned and his cheeks puffed out. Frank jerked to the side just in time to avoid most of the spittle that flew out of the guy's mouth.

Frank reached out and grabbed the man's right wrist and yanked up, then down. The man screamed as the jagged edges of his broken bones grated against one another.

Frank pulled out a knife. "The bones are already broken. Shouldn't be tough to cut through. Then there's just a mess of veins and nerves and meat and flesh. You want to see what it's like to hold your own severed arm?"

"Enough," the man said through clenched teeth. "I'll talk. I'll talk."

The left side of Frank's mouth turned upward in a smile. He broke the guy down fast. While we'd seen some turn faster, we expected this guy to last a few rounds before caving in.

Frank let go and the man pulled his broken arm to his chest. Cradled it with his left arm. He let out a couple sobs, then wiped his eyes dry. Tears stained his cheeks and settled into his thin facial hair.

"What do you want to know?" he said.

"I want to know what you were doing at the bus stop," I said.

He licked his lips and leaned back in the chair and let out a loud exhale. "Got a cigarette?"

I looked at Frank and nodded. Frank reached into his pocket and pulled out a soft pack. He tapped the open end against his palm and retrieved three cigarettes. He lit two and handed one to the man. Rolled the third across the table to me. I tucked it behind my ear, choosing to save it for later.

"The bus stop is where the pick up was going to be made," the guy said.

"What pick up?" I said.

He shifted his eyes from the table to me. "The kid."

I felt Frank's eyes settle on me, but I didn't look back at him. "What kid?"

The man's facial expression changed. The pain and anger lifted, and a bemused look crossed his face. "What did you pick me up for, man?"

"We've been tracking you guys for months. We've got you for drugs, guns, and smuggling terrorists in and out of the country."

He threw his head back and laughed. The spasmodic motion of his body jolted his arm a few inches more than was comfortable and he scrunched his face in pain. After a few seconds he steadied himself and said, "OK, you're onto something with the guns and drugs. They pay well. But the terrorists in and out, you're way off."

"What then?" Frank said. "And what about the kids?"

"Is that all you got? You think these people entered and exited the country alone?" The smile returned to Pablo's face.

"Stop fucking with us," Frank said. "What are you talking about the—"

"Frank," I said. "He's talking about us being way off. This isn't a terrorist cell."

Pablo's eyebrows arched up into his forehead and his smile widened. He looked between me and Frank and nodded vigorously.

I continued, "They're child smugglers. He was at the bus stop today because he was going to kidnap a child."

"You son of a bitch." Frank charged the man and punched him three times in the head, rendering him unconscious.

By the time I got across the table, Frank had backed up. He looked down at the bloodied face of Pablo and shook his hand, which was equally covered in blood. I couldn't tell if it was all Pablo's, or if Frank had split a knuckle or two.

"Well, that was tactful," I said.

"I got kids, Jack."

"I know."

"Christ," Frank said as he stepped around Pablo and made his way toward the door. "What now?"

I followed Frank out into the lobby. The door slammed behind us, echoing through the room. The doctor looked up and saw us and opened his door.

"Need me to do anything?" he asked.

"Smelling salts," I said. "And check his arm. Might need to be set again."

The doctor reached for his bag. "That's why I went with the air cast," he said with a smile.

Frank stood in the middle of the room with his hands on his hips and his head leaned back.

"You need to get it together," I said. "I'll have you pulled from this."

"I'm good. I'm good."

"OK," I said. "We need to get some more information out of him. Now, I don't think he's going to give up anyone else. At least, not yet. But maybe we can get the location of where they are keeping these kids."

"You sure about this? What if he's jerking us around?" Frank said.

"That's why we need the location. We can verify it in person, then come back and hammer on him some more, and then we'll lead a raid on the place."

Frank nodded as the doctor emerged from the interrogation room.

"He's ready for you guys again," the doctor said.

I grabbed Frank by his shoulders. "Let me do the talking." Then I pushed him toward the room. I wanted Frank to enter first, figuring it would cause the man to feel a little more unsettled.

Pablo was conscious when we entered, but he looked confused.

"Where are you keeping them?" I said.

"Who?" Pablo said.

"The kids."

"In a house."

"Where?"

"Northern Virginia. Suburbs."

"Which one?"

"I don't know the name of the neighborhood. Spring Street. Ninth house on the right."

"Going which way?"

"You can only enter from the north."

I looked at Frank and he nodded.

"Good enough." I stepped to the door and pulled it open. Turned back and saw Frank stop in front of Pablo and lean over and drive his fist into the side of the man's face again.

"Was that necessary?" I said.

Frank looked at me, then at Pablo, then back at me. "Yes."

Visit https://ltryan.com/jack-noble for purchasing information.

Take Down

Deep State

Rachel Hatch Series

Drift

Downburst

Fever Burn

Smoke Signal

Firewalk

Whitewater

Aftershock

Whirlwind

Mitch Tanner Series

The Depth of Darkness

Into The Darkness

Deliver Us From Darkness

Cassie Quinn Series

Path of Bones

Whisper of Bones

Symphony of Bones

Etched in Shadow

Concealed in Shadow

Blake Brier Series

Unmasked

Unleashed

Uncharted

Drawpoint

Contrail

Affliction Z Series

Affliction Z: Patient Zero

Affliction Z: Abandoned Hope

Affliction Z: Descended in Blood

Affliction Z: Fractured (Part 1)

Affliction Z: Fractured (Part 2)

ABOUT THE AUTHOR

L.T. Ryan is a *Wall Street Journal, USA Today* and Amazon international best-selling author. The new age of publishing offered L.T. the opportunity to blend his passions for creating, marketing, and technology to reach audiences with his popular Jack Noble series.

Living in central Virginia with his wife, the youngest of his three daughters, and their three dogs, L.T. enjoys staring out his window at the trees and mountains while he should be writing, as well as reading, hiking, running, and playing with gadgets. See what he's up to at https://ltryan.com.

facebook.com/LTRyanAuthor

instagram.com/ltryanauthor